THE SAGE OF SAIGON 2:
THE PHILIPPINE CONNECTION

STEVE CREWS

Order this book online at www.trafford.com
or email orders@trafford.com

Most Trafford titles are also available
at major online book retailers.

© Copyright 2016 Steve Crews.
All rights reserved. No part of this publication
may be reproduced, stored in a retrieval system, or
transmitted, in any form or by any means, electronic,
mechanical, photocopying, recording, or otherwise,
without the written prior permission of the author.

Print information available on the last page.

ISBN: 978-1-4907-7415-2 (sc)
ISBN: 978-1-4907-7417-6 (hc)
ISBN: 978-1-4907-7416-9 (e)

Library of Congress Control Number: 2016908846

Because of the dynamic nature of the Internet, any web
addresses or links contained in this book may have changed
since publication and may no longer be valid. The views
expressed in this work are solely those of the author and do
not necessarily reflect the views of the publisher, and the
publisher hereby disclaims any responsibility for them.

Any people depicted in stock imagery provided by Thinkstock
are models,and such images are being used for illustrative
purposes only. Certain stock imagery © Thinkstock.

*Trafford rev. 07/12/2016*

www.trafford.com
North America & international
toll-free: 1 888 232 4444 (USA & Canada)
fax: 812 355 4082

ALSO BY STEVE CREWS:

SURVIVING BIEN HOA

A DEATH IN KOREA AND THE SEARCH FOR ANSWERS

THE SAGE OF SAIGON

This novel is a work of fiction even though some dates, events and some information used are facts. Any resemblance between the fictional characters used in this book and any real people is purely coincidental.

Happiness is not the absence of conflict but the ability to cope with it.
- Henry Ford -

PROLOGUE

   Shortly before First Lieutenant Tom Ross was medically evacuated from Vietnam, disaster struck in the Philippines. Back-to-back typhoons destroyed the roads, rail lines and bridges between Clark Air Base and Manila as well as in other parts of the country. Hundreds of people were killed and thousands were left homeless. What used to be a trip of a little over an hour from Clark to Manila, now took over four hours.
   To make matters even worse, political instability caused the president of the country to declare martial law. A curfew was put into effect from 11 p.m. to 5 a.m. The Philippine Constabulary and military forces were authorized to shoot anyone on sight who was carrying a weapon or breaking the law in some way during those hours of darkness.

The shocking news of his wife's violent death in a bus explosion, caused by a land mine detonated by the Viet Cong, had brought Lieutenant Ross to the brink of a complete mental breakdown. Years later, his condition would be given a new name, Post Traumatic Stress Disorder, PTSD.

Only the intervention of his congressman from Oklahoma and the former commanding general of Military Assistance Command, Vietnam, kept Lieutenant Ross from being medically discharged. He had asked for their help and the help of the medical staff in the psychiatric ward of the base hospital to help him return to duty.

He was determined to find out who was responsible for the deaths of Genevieve Ferrand Ross, his wife of only a few days, and her uncle, Pierre Ferrand.

It was under these less-than-favorable circumstances that Air Force Office of Special Investigations agent Tom Ross, began a new quest, an adventurous and extremely dangerous journey that would put him in harms way once again.

CHAPTER 1

"NOOOOOO!" he screamed, loud enough to wake the dead.
The small bus carrying thirty-six civilian passengers lifted high into the air as a huge explosion occurred directly under it, ripping it to pieces, flinging burning chunks of metal and body parts in all directions. After the flames and smoke diminished, the largest piece visible was a charred and mangled steel frame. It was turned on its side, with lots of black smoke billowing upwards towards the blue sky from six burning tires.
First Lieutenant Tom Ross' heart was virtually pounding in his chest as if he'd just completed the annual mile-and-a-half aerobics run that was required of everyone in the Air Force. He was sweating profusely as

he sat up in his hospital bed. He felt helpless, unable to do anything as he watched the bus carrying his half-French, half-Vietnamese wife, her French uncle and dozens of innocent Vietnamese civilians, explode in a giant fireball.

Ross was experiencing another terrifying nightmare, brought on by the newspaper article he'd read that had been written about the gruesome atrosity. A large black and white photograph accompanied the story, having been taken at the scene shortly after the terrible explosion. The haunting image of that horrific sight was forever etched in his memory.

"What the hell was that?" the young male physician assistant asked his co-worker.

He'd been sitting behind the nurse's station desk, reading a paperback novel to pass the time. They were in between the scheduled rounds and he had a few minutes to kill. It had been a quiet and somewhat boring shift so far. The loud scream had made him jump, almost tipping his chair over backwards. He put the book down while looking over at the ward nurse.

"Oh shit, it's him again! Let's go!" the older female registered nurse yelled as she tossed the nail file down onto the desk top. She jumped out of her chair that was near another desk a few feet away from his. The terrifying scream had made her jump too, almost causing her to lose her grip on the nail file she'd been using. So much for a quiet, uneventful night, she thought.

The two of them quickly ran down the hall with the RN leading the way. This had happened before during their overnight shift and she knew exactly which room to head for. The janitorial services people had already waxed and buffed the light green linoleum floor to a high gloss which shone brightly under the long sets of fluorescent lights that lit up the hallway twenty-four hours a day.

The nurse pushed the patient's door open, flicked on the bright fluorescent lights and rushed over to the side of Ross' bed. She and the PA knew immediately what had caused the bloodcurdiling scream and hoped it would be the last time she ever heard it. It was upsetting to her nerves and even more so to some of the other patients in the ward.

Their patient looked terrible. Beads of perspiration covered his face, which was all scrunched up as if he was wincing in a lot of pain. His sheets and pillowcase were thoroughly soaked with his sweat. He was sitting up, staring across the room at the wall next to the door. His eyes were wide open with a look of terror in them, as if he had just seen a ghost.

He kept mumbling, "Genevieve, Genevieve," over and over again as giant sobs shook his entire body and tears slid down his cheeks. The twenty-seven year old patient was five-nine, one hundred sixty-five pounds, with curly brown hair and hazel eyes. Now he looked much older and more haggard than they had ever seen him before. To the RN and PA both, his overall appearance was the epitome of misery. It was clear that he was in a state of great emotional distress.

The last thing that Ross heard before Genevieve's life-like image faded away, was her soft voice speaking Vietnamese, her beautiful French-accented words that meant, "I love you very much forever."

The nurse woke Ross up by shaking him several times and calling out his name, bringing him back to the world of the living. After he was totally awake and calmed down, the PA assisted him in changing into dry pajamas and then helped the RN change the bedding. After they were sure that Ross was all right, they got him back into bed. He quickly fell back asleep after he apologized for disturbing everyone again. The incident had embarrassed him quite a bit, even more than it had the last time it happened.

An entry was made on the form at the end of the bed so his doctor would know that he had the same terrible nightmare again. They figured it was the same one since he called out to Genevieve as he'd done before. Then the nurse and physician assistant went around the ward assuring the other patients who'd been awakened by the sudden noisy outburst that everything was OK now.

"Another night of mental hell for the poor guy," the nurse commented to her co-worker after returning to their desks.

"Yeah, I kind of feel sorry for him," came the reply.

Neither one of them had paid any attention to the folded-up newspaper on the nightstand next to Ross' bed. It was the one he'd been given in Saigon when he was informed about what had happened to his wife and her uncle.

The haunting nightmares inexplicably stopped after two months. Ross couldn't figure out why, nor could his psychiatrist, Doctor Melvin Edwards. That was a big relief to them both. Ross was eager to return to work again and knew that the nightmares had been part of the problem that kept him from doing so. As for his doctor, that was a positive sign of progress, of a return to normalcy.

In order to remain in the Air Force and not receive a medical discharge, Ross had to be cleared by his doctor. To stay in the same career field, he also had to meet one other condition. The local Air Force Office of Special Investigations detachment commander would only allow him to work as a member of his organization if he agreed to undergo psychoanalysis. If everything went well, then Ross could return to being an AFOSI agent again, allowed to carry a weapon and work off base if a case required it.

Doctor Edwards was a full-bird colonel. His medical specialty was psychiatry, the branch of medicine that deals with mental, emotional, or behavioral disorders. He was a very busy man. In addition to being a department head, he also treated patients and mentored a couple of interns.

The office of the fifty-two year old doctor was on the fifth floor of the 13th Air Force Regional Medical Center at Clark Air Base. It was a large white building with a few clinics located in some nearby single-story buildings. The main hospital had a long circular driveway in front with spaces reserved for handicap parking, taxis and a bus stop for the civilian-operated base shuttle bus. There were two large parking lots on either side of the long main entrance drive, between the hospital and the well-traveled road that ran in front of it.

The emergency room entrance was on the right side of the facility, looking at it from the front, with ample parking nearby for patients and staff. Both the front main entrance and ER entrance had awnings over them to help keep everyone dry as they entered or exited the building. The rainy season here produced heavy tropical downpours, especially when a typhoon was anywhere in the area. The rainy season lasted for six months as did the dry season.

At one hundred eighty pounds, the six-foot two, silver-haired doctor looked lean and trim in his uniform. Most of the time he wore a white smock over it, what some people called a lab coat. He found that by covering up the silver eagles on his broad shoulders, patients seemed less intimidated and opened up to him more, especially the enlisted military patients, who were more prone to be rank-conscious.

Doctor Edwards stood at the window of his office, peering through the dusty venetian blinds. His focus was on the old NCO Club that was across the street and off to his right, a little ways down the road. It was scheduled to be torn down soon. He'd heard that the base was going to get a new NCO Club, a new commissary and a new Airmen's Club too. He knew it wasn't just another rumor going around, of which there always seemed to be a few. Recently, a fellow doctor had told him that the base newspaper, The Philippine Flyer, had published an article about all the new construction work that would be starting in the next few weeks. There was even talk of a second runway to be built sometime in the future.

He wondered when the old Officer's Club would be torn down and replaced. It had been built many years ago where Fort Stotsenburg once stood, near the parade grounds next to the base housing area commonly referred to as Colonel's Row. There had been no mention of that. Oh well, that was someone else's problem, he thought. His problem was much more pressing than that. Much more so.

He'd recently been informed, while attending an important meeting hosted by the commanding general of 13th Air Force, that American prisoners of war held captive in North Vietnam, would soon be released. They would be flown from Hanoi to Clark Air Base in Air Force C-141 Starlifter cargo planes. The aircraft would be outfitted with comfort pallets that contained a restroom, coffee maker, refrigerator and the type of food preparation ovens similar to the ones found in major airline galleys. The planes would also be fitted with comfortable airline-type seats for the special passengers. Some of the aircraft would be configured to carry rows of stretchers, with medical personnel aboard, to care for the seriously injured, according to the general. The former prisoners of war would be staying at Clark for at least a few days, their length of stay being dependant upon their physical and mental condition.

They would all get to go on a shopping spree and get new uniforms in the Clothing Sales store and whatever they wanted in the Base Exchange. The BX would be closed for one day to everyone else so they could have the place all to themselves and buy anything their hearts desired.

The general also mentioned that it would be up to the medical staff of the base hospital to give the newly-freed men thorough and complete physical exams and to perform any medical procedures, including surgery, if necessary. That also included dental exams and oral surgery as well. They knew that many of the former POWs had been tortured by the North Vietnamese and some had been injured when ejecting from their aircraft. They were expecting to see some men in pretty rough condition, those at the general's briefing were told.

Doctor Edwards and his staff were responsible for giving each former POW a thorough mental evaluation. Some of them might want to continue with their military service and would need to be evaluated both mentally and physically to determine if that choice was still feasible.

They would be given top priority over regular patients so they could return to the U.S. as soon as possible. That meant Doctor Edwards would have to delegate some of his responsibilities to others on his staff and maybe even to the two interns working under his supervision as well.

With so much to plan for, he decided to hold a staff meeting shortly after returning from the 13th Air Force Headquarters. The office across the hall from his was used for staff meetings.

"We're having this short-notice staff meeting in place of our regularly scheduled one," Doctor Edwards began, "because we're about to be tasked with a very important job which I just learned about from the 13th Air Force commander."

He paused and looked around the small table at the four people that made up his staff. He, along with two of them, would soon participate in an historic event, the care of former POWs from the war in Vietnam.

"As you all know, not only am I the head of this medical clinic but I also treat patients and supervise interns."

The two interns sat to his left and the two permanently-assigned Air Force psychiatrists sat to his right. Doctor Edwards sat at the head of the table on the end farthest from the room's only window. There was a large metal pitcher full of ice water at the center of the table and everyone had a tall glass of ice water in front of them, along with the note pads and pens they normally brought to these meetings.

"In the very near future, we're going to be screening some former POWs that will be flying in here from Hanoi. They will become our top priority as soon as they arrive and will remain so as long as they're here."

"How long will they be staying here?" his second-in-command, Doctor (Major) David Longstreet asked.

"That depends on their physical and mental condition," Edwards replied. "There's no set time frame that I'm aware of. What I want to tell you now is that I'm going to have to delegate my patient workload to the two interns so I can focus on the former POWs. At the present time, I have two patients under my care. Mr. Lawrence, I'm assigning Airman First Class Christopher Rodgers to you, starting tomorrow. I'll go over his case with you today so stick around after the meeting. We'll be having another meeting at a later date to go over things more thoroughly after I get more information on the POWs. Any questions, Mr. Lawrence?"

The intern sitting closest to him replied soon thereafter, "No sir."

"OK. And Miss Edwards, you stick around after the meeting too and I'll go over your new case with you as well. Any questions?"

He could see a concerned look on the female intern's face and knew from past experience that she'd ask at least one question. She was always asking him questions, which was a good thing in his opinion.

"Just one, sir. Who will my patient be?" she inquired, somewhat tentatively.

"You'll be getting a challenging case too but one in which I have complete faith in your ability to handle. First Lieutenant Tom Ross will be all yours starting first thing tomorrow morning. OK?"

"Yes, sir. I'm up for the challenge," she added confidently, her face now broadening into a smile. She welcomed the opportunity to put what she'd learned to the test and help someone who really needed it.

"Good, that's good," Doctor Edwards

replied.  He paused to take a big swallow of ice water from the tall sweating glass in front of him.  "Like I said earlier, as more information about our new patients comes in, we'll have another meeting and go over all the details.  Well, that's all I have for now."

Looking over at Doctor Longstreet and Doctor (Captain) Carl Kingston, the other staff psychiatrist, he said, "Dave, Carl, you guys can go.  I've got to go over my two patient cases with the interns before I turn 'em loose.  Unless either of you have any questions, I'll see you both later."

Neither Longstreet nor Kingston asked a question and they left the meeting room together.  The small staff was a tight-knit group and Doctor Edwards liked to conduct informal, almost laid-back staff meetings without the military formalities of the room being called to attention when he walked in. With just the five of them and no one else present, he could do things that way.  His staff appreciated his personal touch when it came to things like that and so did the patients in the ward.  He spent the next thirty minutes with the two interns, giving them the information they needed.  Then they all left the meeting room.

Back in his own office, Doctor Edwards stood at the window and watched a base shuttle bus pull up to the bus stop close to the front entrance of the hospital.  He noticed that many of the passengers had their faces up to their open windows, hoping to catch a breeze.  The buses weren't air conditioned and every window was open all the way.  It was another cloudless, hot, sunny day in the middle of the dry season.  There were only two seasons here, unlike the four back in the States.  It was either hot and dry or hot and wet.  The rainy season was still a few months away.

He stepped away from the window and returned to his large cluttered desk, picking up the medical record of First Lieutenant Tom Ross. He'd decided, but only reluctantly so, to turn the treatment plan of grief counseling that he had begun and the psychoanalysis that was also required, over to one of his trusted interns. He set the record in his OUT basket, where she would pick it up in the morning.

His workload was about to increase to the point where he really didn't have a choice but to delegate some of it to others. The other two officers would be very busy as well so he couldn't burden either one of them with another case. The good thing about all this was, he was totally confident in the abilities of this particular intern that had been assigned to treat Lieutenant Ross. She was his daughter.

A once-in-a-lifetime set of circumstances that was all due to the arrival of former POWs at Clark Air Base, was about to change the life of Tom Ross in ways that he could never have imagined. His life would be likened to the phoenix, the legendary bird which, according to one account, burned itself to ashes on a pyre and rose alive from the ashes to live again. The old Ross would die with his last nightmare. A new persona would emerge from months of counseling and psychoanalysis. Freed from the guilt he felt for not being able to prevent his wife's death in Vietnam, he would learn to live again, in the Philippines.

CHAPTER 2

Business had gone down quite a bit at the Newport docks on the Saigon River. Ever since the United States pulled out all of its combat troops, far fewer ships were docking there. Mang Binh Hao's scrap metal business was hardly a business at all anymore.

When American and South Vietnamese troops used to do battle against the North Vietnamese and Viet Cong, copious amounts of artillery shell casings, blown-up armored personnel carriers, jeeps, tanks, trucks and helicopters once used by South Vietnamese military forces, were loaded aboard ships at Newport, scrap metal for export to other countries.

With the departure of almost half-a-million Americans over the past few years and the changes in South Vietnam's military strategy, the scrap metal business suffered greatly. Now most South Vietnamese military units were content with a strategy called "defending-in-place," remaining in their base camps and around large population centers. That allowed North Vietnamese units to take over large areas of sparsely populated territory. Neither side fought major battles as they had in the past when American military forces were present.

The leaders in the North were building up their forces for a future all-out offensive. Even the Viet Cong seemed to be taking a break, compared to years past. It was like the proverbial "calm before the storm."

To make up for the loss of income from the scrap metal business, the owner of the Gulf of Lion Shipping Company, Mang Binh Hao, decided to ramp up his drug smuggling business. While some of the large-scale battles of the past had interrupted the flow of opium and marijuana from the Golden Triangle into South Vietnam, this somewhat peaceful interlude provided an opportunity that he seized upon with a renewed passion. The flow of drugs was picking up again, even though Hao was forced to find a new buyer.

The recent death of the drug kingpin in Singapore had caused a big loss of income. He and Hao had been doing a lot of business over the past few years. The government of that former British crown colony, located at the southern end of the Malay Peninsula, had begun executing drug dealers and that included Hao's buyer. The death penalty for drug dealers had put an abrupt end to Mang Binh Hao's very lucrative business in Singapore.

"Which port are we headed for today, Mr.

Hao?" the ship's captain asked, as Hao's favorite cargo vessel, Lady of the Seas, pulled away from the Newport dock.

"Manila is our destination. We will dock at pier five in North Harbor. Have someone let me know when we get there. I'll be in my cabin," he stated, somewhat hurriedly.

Hao quickly left the bridge and headed directly for his stately cabin, the largest and most lavishly furnished one by far. All of the cabinets, his desk and both dressers were made of hand-crafted teak. His bed's frame and headboard were made of solid Philippine mahogany, as was the ornately carved wet bar with hand-tooled roses that adorned the front. The sink faucets and showerhead were all gold-plated and the cabin even had a walk-in closet nearly as large as the huge marble-walled shower stall.

As soon as the ship's captain was certain that Hao was nowhere near, he engaged the first officer in conversation. They were both French and had worked for Hao for several years now.

"So, Jean, want to make a little wager?" the captain, Maurice Lambert asked. The fifty-eight year old had been in charge of Lady of the Seas for a little over three years now. The previous captain had mysteriously disappeared just before he'd been hired.

"You know me, sir. If there is money to be made, I'm in," Jean Gaboriau replied with a grin. Two years younger and two inches shorter than the six-foot-tall captain, First Officer Gaboriau was also divorced and had some spare money to gamble with. The ship's crew were all well-paid. "What is it you'd like to wager on and how much?"

"Have you ever noticed," the captain began, "that each time we leave Saigon, the young women who board the ship with Hao are not seen again, either getting off the ship with him at any port we visit or back at Newport when we return?"

Jean contemplated those facts for a moment and then he frowned slightly, causing his brown mustache to droop over the corners of his mouth. His bright blue eyes lit up as he finally came up with a reply.

"Now that you mention it, you're right! I never gave it much thought before, probably because I'm always so busy whenever we dock. I too have seen some of them come aboard with Hao, but never have I seen any of them leave when he does. Mon Dieu! You are not suggesting..."

Maurice shook his balding head up and down and smiled at Jean. "Oui, mon ami. I'll bet you a thousand francs that Hao is disposing of them somehow. Maybe even feeding them to the fish, if you know what I mean."

"But how can you be so sure? How can you prove it?" Jean was still not one hundred percent convinced.

"Face the facts, Jean," Maurice said, lowering his voice a little. "This one who came on board today is no different. I'll bet you that neither of us see the young woman walk off this ship. Is it a bet?"

Jean shook his head no, stepping a little closer to the captain who was now at the helm. "No sir, I will not bet on a losing proposition. As much as I hate to think that Hao is killing these women or having someone do it for him, I think you're right."

A strained look then appeared on his face as he considered the dilemma he now found himself in. "What should we do? I mean, what if that is exactly what has been happening and may even happen again?"

"We keep our mouths shut and our eyes open, that's what we do," Maurice replied. He looked his first officer in the eyes until he was sure he had made his point very clear. "As long as Hao doesn't think that we suspect anything, we have nothing to worry about. We have no real proof of any wrongdoing to give to the authorities anyway, so it's best to say nothing. Agreed?"

Jean nodded his consent. "Yes, you are right of course. We have no proof, no evidence, only our suspicions."

The helmsman then returned to the pilothouse from the head and took over his position from the captain. The coffee he drank earlier that morning had needed draining. He had no idea what the two Frenchmen had been talking about. He didn't speak their language at all as he was from Scotland and they always spoke to him in English. The ship had an international crew, as was the case with most ships of this type. The only difference was, this ship always returned to port with fewer people on board than it started out with.

For a man in his late forties, Mang Binh Hao could still move quickly. He went down the steps leading to his cabin as nimbly as a younger deckhand would. The reason for his urgency became apparent as soon as he opened the door to his home-away-from-home. At five-four and one hundred twenty pounds, the brown-eyed, brown-haired man who loved to dress in brown, could have easily been mistaken for one of the Asian deckhands he employed.

His current concubine for this long sea voyage was laying naked under the expensive purple satin sheets, waiting for him in the new heated water bed that he had someone install for him as soon as he found out about their existance.

"It's not the size of the ship that matters most to a woman," a friend of his had recently told him, "but the motion of the ocean."

So as soon as he could get one, there being none anywhere in South Vietnam that he could find, he had it assembled in his cabin. A king-size bed for a king-size ego. That's where he had his first heated water bed sexual experience, on his ship out at sea. The water bed added even more motion to the ocean and more zest to his love life.

His beautiful, young, teenage concubine from Hong Kong was a nymphomaniac to begin with. Now, on this large heated water bed at sea, she was absolutely insatiable and her sexual appetite wore him out. The drugs he had given her and the heated water bed that she just loved might have had something to do with that.

It seemed to Hao, that whenever young women used heroin, it somehow increased their lustful desires. That was why he provided them with a limitless supply of the stuff. It was a derivative of opium and was a strongly physiologically addictive narcotic. His concubines became drug addicts, totally under his control and he became completely immersed in the carnal pleasures of their soft, lithe, young bodies.

That's not what made him a monster though. It was what he did to them after he was through with them that made him so shockingly evil. Whenever he decided that he wanted a new mistress in his life, he simply got them doped up on heroin and then tossed them overboard in the warm, shark-infested waters of the South China Sea in the dark of night and out in the middle of nowhere. Under the influence of drugs, the young women never realized what was happening to them. To Mang Binh Hao, they were a "loose end." They could share his bed but never his secrets. People died whenever he decided to tie up "loose ends." That's what made him so evil and dangerous.

Bhoy Santos had just finished paying his respects to the many ancestors he had in the old Chinese cemetery. It was located between Jose Abad Santos Street and Bonifacio Avenue, a couple of miles north of his home in Binondo, metro Manila. He climbed into the front passenger seat of the multi-colored and highly-decorated jeepney. His personal touch was the silver horse hood ornament. It was one of several jeepneys he owned. With brown eyes, brown hair and being an average size man, standing only five feet four and weighing one hundred twenty-five pounds, he blended in well with the men he traveled with. The only thing that distinguished him from the others with him now was his age. He was forty-five years old and he hired men no older than thirty.

His relatives had lived in and around Chinatown, in the suburb of Manila named Binondo, for hundreds of years. After the Spanish built the walled city of Intramuros at the mouth of the Pasig River in the late 1500s, trade between the Spaniards and Chinese began to flourish. Chinese traders were eventually allowed to build a settlement across from Intramuros on the north side of the Pasig River.

The Chinese community that grew in Binondo underwent several changes over the years as many of the men began to have Philippino wives, converted to Catholicism and adopted a Christian name. The offspring of a Chinese father and native mother were called mestizos.

Bhoy Santos came from a Chinese-Philippino mestizo family of wealthy business people. His grandfather on his mother's side of the family had once been Chief of Manila Harbor Customs, working directly for the president of the country. He became very wealthy over the many years he held that job, mainly because of the bribes he accepted from many ship captains who wished to introduce many forms of contraband into the country.

Bhoy Santos, on the other hand, was the buyer of some of that contraband, specifically marijuana, opium and heroin. And, like a true gangster, he ran a very lucrative protection racket as well.

He and Mang Binh Hao had a few things in common. They were both in their forties. They both had ancestors that had been Chinese traders, having come from the southern Chinese coastal province of Fujian. Also, they could both speak Chinese and English and they were both very ruthless in their handling of any obstacles that stood in their way. That explained why there were six armed men riding in the back side-facing bench seats of the jeepney with Bhoy Santos. They were with him almost everywhere he went, today being no exception.

Over the past few years, Mang Binh Hao, who was born Chinese but Vietnamized his name, had been traveling to Hong Kong, Taiwan, Singapore, Manila, Guam and Hawaii to do business. He sold tons of scrap metal as well as lots of black tar opium, heroin and marijuana. He laundered his money in the international banking community in various Asian cities.

Hao was married to Ling Thi Xuan, the half-sister of the South Vietnamese president's wife. He helped President Trung Ho

Quoch and his wife, Ly Than Mai, with several multi-million dollar corruption scemes, especially the ones in which he put large amounts of money into the Quoch bank accounts in Hong Kong and Singapore. He also assisted the president of South Vietnam by making silent-partner investments in Taiwan, Guam and Hawaii. To say that Mang Binh Hao was well-connected would be an understatement.

That was no help to him in the Philippine islands however. With that country now being ruled with an iron fist under martial law, he had to go through Bhoy Santos in order to keep that market for drugs open. The person Hao had previously done business with in Manila had been jailed by President Marcos as a "subversive." Santos had since taken over from him.

Hao was aware that Americans had many military bases in the Philippines. There was one on Mactan Island, near Cebu. There were two fairly close together near the city of Olongapo, Subic Bay and Cubi Point. The largest one was in central Luzon, the huge Clark Air Base, with Camp O'Donnell north of there. Then there was Wallace Air Station near the Lingayan Gulf, also on Luzon and east of there, high up in the mountains near the city of Baguio was Camp John Hay. The Americans also had some troops in Manila at the JUSMAG (Joint U.S. Military Assistance Group) compound and their embassy, as well as at the international airport and a few scattered elsewhere as military advisors to the Philippine military establishment. Since some American GIs were still using drugs as their troops in Vietnam had done, Hao needed to continue doing business with them, along with drug-using Philippinos. That's why the meeting with Bhoy Santos in North Harbor, Manila was so important.

CHAPTER 3

    Ross woke up feeling like he was in limbo, a state of uncertainty, and he couldn't figure out why. It was a strange feeling that he wasn't used to and it bothered him. He began putting his uniform on again, just like he'd done hundreds of times before, but unlike before, he wasn't going to work. He was headed for the hospital to see a doctor. He still wasn't used to doing that either, even after a couple of appointments.
    He felt fine physically but he didn't feel good about having to go through a period of grief counseling and "psychotherapy" sessions, as he called it, in order to be returned to normal duty. That meant his future was still very much in question and that **really** bothered him. He liked being in control of his own life, his own future, but right now, it was out of his

hands.

Big deal. So he'd had some nightmares and disturbed some other patients in the ward he'd been in at the hospital when he first got there. He'd told everyone he was sorry. Wasn't that enough?

Before leaving his room in the Bachelor Officer's Quarters, he took one last look in the mirror to make sure his name tag and ribbons on his short sleeve blue uniform shirt were on straight. He checked once more to make sure the ribbons representing the National Defense Service Medal, Vietnam Service Medal, Air Force Overseas Short Tour ribbon, Air Force Longevity Service Award, Republic of Vietnam Gallantry Cross with Palm, Republic of Vietnam Campaign Medal with one oak leaf cluster and the Air Force Good Conduct Medal were in the correct order. All good.

Then, just before stepping away from the mirror, he paused to admire his shiny new silver "railroad tracks" that were the bars of a Captain he'd recently received with his promotion. "Captain Ross," he said to himself. That sounded so much better than First Lieutenant Ross, he thought. That part of his life made him very happy, but only that part. After he found, then killed the man or men directly responsible for the death of his wife, he'd be even happier. That was always in the back of his mind.

He checked in at the reception desk of the clinic he'd been to before and took a seat in the small waiting room. He was the only person there and for that he was very thankful. He didn't want to be seen here. In his mind, he was in the "Psycho Ward" and that was embarrassing to him. He looked around and saw there were six brown, rattan, high-backed chairs with matching brown seat cushions and a couple of lightweight rattan coffee tables with an assortment of magazines on them. Had there been a window or two with curtains, it would have seemed like a room in someone's house. He was in the seat closest to the door and closed his eyes for a few seconds, wishing he was anywhere but here.

A pleasant-sounding female voice startled him and brought him back to the here and now. He'd begun to daydream of better, happier times back in Vietnam with his wife, Genevieve.

"Hello Captain Ross. My name is Maribel Edwards. I've been assigned as your counselor. How are you today?"

He politely stood up and shook the outstretched hand she offered. It was a lot smaller and softer than his and he took care to not squeeze it too hard. She was not the person he was expecting to see and the huge difference caught him by surprise. The doctor he'd seen before was a white male, fifty-two years old, six feet tall with silver hair and weighed about one hundred eighty pounds. That and brown eyes was a fair description of Doctor Melvin Edwards, Colonel, U.S. Air Force.

The person he was facing now was definitely not Doctor Edwards. This young lady, he guessed, was in her early twenties, around five feet five inches tall and he bet himself she weighed no more than one hundred ten pounds soaking wet. She had slightly almond-shaped, not-quite-round, brown eyes, long dark brown hair and an engaging smile which showed off her perfectly-alligned, pearly-white teeth, something Ross couldn't help but notice. She was an attractive young woman, no doubt about it. Definitely not Doctor Edwards, not by a long shot.

"OK," he managed to reply, still a little bit surprised. "Are you a doctor too?" She was wearing a white coat like one, with her name tag on it, but for some reason he just felt like asking.

"No, not yet. I'm an intern here. I'm a graduate student at U.P., the University of the Philippines, studying to become a board-certified psychiatrist. I work under the supervision of Doctor Edwards, who you saw before. He'll be monitoring my work and your progress."

She shifted his medical records from one hand to the other, then told him to follow her to an office down the long corridor. As he trailed behind her, he thought that even if she wasn't really a doctor yet, she sure looked the part, and even acted like one too.

Maribel stood just inside her office door and offered Ross the only chair in the room that wasn't behind her gray metal desk. It was a very plain-looking office, with no diplomas or personal photographs on the walls or on the desk. White venetian blinds covered the only window in the room. It was all very antiseptic-looking to Ross. He guessed that she had been given this particular office to use because she wasn't a full-time resident doctor here, therefore she rated only a second-rate office. These thoughts were a reflection of his mood about being here today. He'd rather have been just about anywhere else.

"So why am I not seeing Doctor Edwards today?" Ross asked, hoping for a reasonable explanation.

"He and some other doctors," she began, "are working extra-long hours now because of many new patients who just arrived. He told me that he felt I was ready to take on a new patient. Don't worry. He'll pop in from time to time to see how things are going," she assured him.

26

Having recently seen the local TV news broadcasts of the Armed Forces Radio and Television Service and editions of Pacific Stars and Stripes newspapers, Ross was well aware, as most Americans were by now, of the recent arrivals of American POWs from Hanoi. No doubt some of them would be in need of at least some psychiatric counseling, he thought. That explained why Doctor Edwards wasn't able to see him now.

"I'd like to discuss a few things with you today since I'm going to be your counselor for awhile, just to make sure I'm not leaving out anything, OK?" She smiled at him, trying to put him at ease. "Feel free to ask me questions at any time," she added.

"OK," he replied, nodding his head and smiling back. Maybe this won't be so bad after all, he thought.

Unknown to Maribel, she wasn't making this initial meeting with Ross any easier for him, because her smile, coming from the face of an attractive young woman who looked somewhat, but not entirely Asian, reminded him of his deceased wife's smile, and he missed his wife a lot. She had been half-French and half-Vietnamese. Unknown to Ross, Maribel was half-American and half-Philippino. There were some similarities between the two women and he couldn't help but notice.

Maribel began again by saying, "You may have heard Doctor Edwards tell you some of the things I'm going to tell you today but it's important that I cover everything, so just bear with me, OK?"

"Fine with me. But, since you're not a doctor, what do I call you, Miss Edwards or Mrs. Edwards?" He really didn't care one way or the other if she was single or married. He just wanted to establish proper etiquette since he'd never addressed a medical intern before.

"Maribel is fine for now," she replied, again with a friendly smile, hoping her patient would feel at ease calling her by her first name.

"OK, Maribel it is. And you can call me by my first name too, when we're in these counseling sessions, instead of Captain Ross. I'm Tom from now on. Are you OK with that?"

"Certainly, Tom, whatever you prefer."

Then her facial expression took on a slightly more serious look as she began to address the issue that brought him here today.

"When someone close to you dies, Tom, there are no simple answers for coping with it. There are usually some common reactions to grief after a loved one dies. One thing you've got to remember is, grief is an emotional process, and a very natural one too, and it takes some time to get through it."

Before she could continue, he asked, "How much time?"

"Well, that differs from person to person. Sometimes it depends on things like coping skills, your religious background, your personality, even your cultural background to some extent."

Maribel paused for a moment and looked at Tom for a sign of understanding. He nodded slightly, then she continued.

"It also depends on your relationship to the person you lost and how their death affects your daily life. It can also depend on, to some degree at least, on how much support you get from your family and friends. So you see, Tom, there are lots of things that cause some people to take longer to get through their grief than others. We're all different that way. And because it's a natural, healthy and perfectly normal response to a loved one's death, grief isn't something to be ashamed of. Unfortunately, because it's sometimes such a difficult and confusing process, that process can last for weeks, months, or even years for some people. Physical and emotional symptoms can also happen and often change during the grieving process. The good thing is, the intensity and frequency of your suffering and pain will lessen over time. The most important thing to remember is, no matter how bad you may feel now, you **will** recover from it."

Ross nodded his head in understanding again when she paused. Giving it some thought, he said, "You mentioned physical and emotional symptoms can also happen. Like what, for example?"

"That's a good question," she replied. "Things like fear, panic, feelings of helplessness, anxiety, even anger. Some people may have feelings of emptiness, loneliness or guilt. One of my professors told us in class one day about a few cases where, believe it or not, people have actually experienced hair loss, headaches, chest pains and shortness of breath. Other examples of physical and emotional symptoms are well-documented, such as people not being able to remember things as well as they used to. Some people have trouble falling asleep at night because they were used to sleeping next to or cuddling with a loved one. There are some cases of people who got tired easily and didn't have the energy to even get out of bed in the morning. There are also cases of people that suffered from sudden mood swings, short attention spans, digestive problems, or, they gained too much weight or lost too much. Some people have even felt that their loved one would come back to them, feeling a sense that their death wasn't real, a sense of denial. So you see, Tom, there is a wide range of symptoms, varrying from person to person."

"Are all those symptoms considered normal?" He hoped his were.

"Oh yes, because nobody is the same. We all grieve differently for different periods of time and experience different symptoms. And, there's no way to predict what you may experience in the future. We can only give you some treatment sessions to help minimize the duration and the amount of symptoms you might experience. With the right treatment, people have gotten through their grieving process sooner and easier than they might have otherwise."

Maribel paused to give Ross a chance to reflect on all the material she'd covered so far. She could tell by the look on his face that he'd been paying attention to her and seemed interested in what she'd just said. At least she hoped that was the case.

"Does that treatment include any type of prescribed medications?" he asked, hoping that he wouldn't be put on anything. He was afraid it might delay his return to duty.

"In some cases it may become necessary. Why?" She noticed the changed look in his eyes when he asked that question. Was it fear maybe?

"I don't want to be medicated at all. I want a clean bill of health so I can get back to work as soon as possible, with no restrictions on travel or use of firearms. My goal is to complete the required counseling sessions and then get on with my life, and the sooner the better," he stated, with a look of determination in his eyes now. And the sooner I can find the SOB that killed my wife, he added to himself.

"I'll do my best to help you reach that goal, Tom, but as this is only 'Day One' in the process, I can't guarantee anything other than that I and Doctor Edwards will do our best to help you. OK?"

He looked into her brown eyes when she said that and he detected nothing but total sincerity. Her pleasant voice and smile, combined with her words, put him at ease. She had earned his trust...so far.

"Sounds good to me," he replied, still a little bit concerned about the possibility of being prescribed some type of medication in the future.

"Are you ready to talk about the personal experiences in your life now? I know it may be painful but to begin making progress, I'm afraid it's going to be necessary."

Ross had been wondering when they were going to get to the point. Let's get this over with, he thought.

"Yes, I'm ready. Let's do this."

Maribel had prepared herself by reading over Doctor Edward's notes on Ross and thoroughly went through his medical records, so she knew a lot about what got her patient to this point in his life. However, she felt there was more she needed to know about him in order to be more helpful in his recovery process.

"As I mentioned earlier," she began, "there are different types of grief and in your case, with your wife being an innocent casualty of war, we call it 'complicated' grief. This type of grief could appear as an inability to express normal reactions of grief or a complete absense of grief. And just the opposite of that, some people might express abnormally intense reactions of grief. That could develop into major depression or alcohol abuse or even drug abuse."

Before she could go on, Ross interjected, "I haven't felt depressed, haven't gotten drunk and haven't done any drugs so I must be doing OK then, right?"

"Yes and no."

Her answer surprised him.

"Your case is somewhat different than most cases we deal with. That's because grief becomes more complicated when a loved one's death is sudden, unexpected, or, unfortunately, very violent, as when your wife ...."

"Genevieve," Ross interjected, making it more personal.

"Yes, Genevieve, became a casualty of war when the Viet Cong blew up the bus she was riding in. And it's an even more traumatic loss when no body is recovered."

Maribel immediately noticed a tenseness come over Ross as soon as she mentioned how his wife, Genevieve, had died so violently. His eyes blinked a few times and he took a longer, deeper breath. Clearly, it was affecting him.

She continued after that brief pause. "Every symptom of grief may be prolonged and even be more intense after this type of traumatic and violent death. It's normal to experience dreams or persistent memories about the event."

"In my case, nightmares, really bad nightmares," Ross volunteered.

"Yes, I'm afraid so and they're well-documented in your medical records. That's something we'd have to work on," Maribel explained, "if they ever return again."

"Sorry to interrupt. Please continue," he said, contritely.

"Yes, well, some people feel an intense sense of guilt, what we call 'survivor's guilt,' feeling that they either should have died instead of their loved one or maybe even that they should have died along with them."

Ross blurted out, as Maribel's last statement struck a nerve, "I told Genevieve and her father that I'd protect her and keep her safe and I failed to do that. So, yes, I feel guilty for not keeping my word."

Maribel noticed the sad look on his face and matching tone of his voice as well. She reminded herself not to get emotionally involved, not to feel sorry for him, to remain a professional grief counselor and help him through this. She directed her next statement towards that end.

"Tom, we both know that things sometimes happen that we have no control over whatsoever. When this guilty feeling continues, you need help overcoming that. That's my area of training and expertise and I'm here to help you."

Ross heard what she said and wondered just how she intended to help him.

"How, specifically, are you going to help me? I mean, how do you get feelings of guilt to stop or feelings like revenge? I'd like to kill the person responsible for killing my wife, her uncle, and all those other innocent people that were on the same bus with them. How?" he repeated. He needed to be convinced.

"As Doctor Edwards and I have told you, losing a loved one suddenly and traumatically presents unexpected challenges. There are five things I'm going to talk about with you that will explain how I'm going to help you, before we begin the psychoanalysis sessions."

"Psychoanalysis?" He'd heard that word before but still wasn't sure exactly what it meant or why it applied to him.

"Yes. That's a method of analyzing psychic phenomena and treating emotional disorders that involves treatment sessions during which you'll be encouraged to talk freely about personal experiences and especially about your early childhood and dreams you've had." Her professor at U.P. would have been proud of her as she told Ross, almost word-for-word, the definition of psychoanalysis, right out of one of her college textbooks.

"Why do I have to go through psychoanalysis?" he asked, with a slightly defensive-sounding tone. "You mean, I have to lay down on a psychiatrist's couch and tell you my life story, going back to my childhood bed-wetting days?" His voice had risen a little bit in volume, sounding as if he was slightly annoyed or upset, which he was. He was trying to maintain his composure but soon realized he wasn't doing it very well.

"No, Tom," she giggled slightly, as she mentally pictured him stretched out on a couch with his hands folded together, babbling on and on about some mundane childhood events. "No couch for you. One of my university professors is a big advocate for working with patients in relaxing settings, sometimes outdoors. That's what we'll do. All I know is what I've been told and that is, as a condition for you to be allowed to carry a weapon again and work off base, you have to undergo psychoanalysis. Then, if Doctor Edwards signs off on the paperwork, you'll be able to return to your unit without any limitations. That's your goal, right? To get back in your old line of work without any limitations?"

"Yes, that's right," he stated emphatically, nodding his head.

"Well, I'm going to do my best to help you reach that goal, Tom. Just bear with me and give me a chance to do my job and work with you, OK? That's all I ask," Maribel concluded. Wow, have I got my work cut out for me, she thought.

"Fair enough," he replied, in a much

calmer and softer-toned voice. He resigned himself to his fate.

Getting things back on track, Maribel stated, "What I'm going to discuss with you today are the five things about grief, in dealing with your particular type of personal tragedy. I know about the horrible way your wife, Genevieve, was killed on that bus in Vietnam and I'm terribly sorry for your loss. I sincerely hope I can help you deal with her death in the best possible way."

"Thank you for that," he responded.

Maribel nodded in reply and then continued. "It's common to experience a sense of unreality, anger, or nightmares. You may blame others for your loss or feel guilty because you didn't have the opportunity to say things you wanted to say to Genevieve. That's the first of the five things. Have you experienced any of these things, Tom?"

"Yes, well, you know all about my nightmares. They're documented in my medical records and there were plenty of witnesses. Those have finally stopped, thank God. I haven't had any in a while now. As for anger, I'm angry at myself for not protecting my wife. I know the Viet Cong are to blame for her death and I'm angry at them too. Genevieve and I were newlyweds so we didn't even take a honeymoon trip yet and yes, there were still some things I didn't get the chance to say to her or have a discussion about, like having kids. I lost the love of my life right when our new life together as a married couple was just getting started. It's hard," he ended, as his eyes welled up with tears and his lips began to quiver.

Unconsciously, Ross had been looking down at his hands in his lap, the right thumb and index finger turning the gold wedding band round and round on his left ring finger, fidgeting nervously. His wife's death had left him single again but he continued to wear the ring anyway. He felt uncomfortable discussing all this with another woman, a woman he'd just met, regardless of her medical background.

Maribel noticed the emotions that finally surfaced and made note of it. She then took up the discussion again, feeling bad for him but knowing she had to continue in order to help him through this.

"I also understand that a photograph of the remains of the bus Genevieve was on was on the front page of a newspaper that was shown to you. Is that right?"

"Yes, that's correct."

"A graphic photograph, along with the newspaper article, are reminders to you of your loss. Those types of things just make healing more difficult. According to witnesses, that's what caused you to pass out and go into a catatonic state, not responding to anyone or anything for a few days. It would be beneficial if you never saw that newspaper again."

"Maribel, no disrespect, but that's where I disagree with you. I've kept a copy of that newspaper to remind me of who is responsible for my wife's death and it keeps me motivated to find them one day." He had a serious, determined look on his face when he said that, with all the conviction of a person who meant to get revenge somehow.

Maribel was a little bit surprised by the statement he'd just made, not expecting him to disagree on such a key issue.

"Revenge, Tom? You're not seriously thinking about returning to Vietnam are you? I mean, how could you possibly get revenge against those who killed your wife and all those other people on that bus, assuming you could even discover which individuals were directly responsible?" To her, his idea seemed preposterous and reflected a need for these counseling sessions.

His reply came only after a very long pause of strained silence. He blinked a few times, cleared his throat with a nervous cough, then said, "I don't know yet, but until I come up with a plan, the photo and newspaper article are my incentives for getting better and getting back to my regular line of work. Let's just call it turning a lemon into lemonade for lack of a better example."

She wrote his statement down on her notepad which was half-full now, then looked up from her desk at him. His hazel eyes looked right back into hers. She could tell that he was very serious about what he'd just said, of that she was certain. It was time for her to regain control of the discussion again and get things back on track.

"OK, well, the third thing I want to talk to you about is that you should try to maintain a daily routine as much as possible. You'll find that it will help in returning a sense of normalcy to your life. You might find it a little difficult in focusing on regular activities at first but, over time, things will improve. I have an idea on how to get started doing that, if you haven't already. Would you feel more comfortable if we conducted our future sessions outdoors, say in one of the nearby picnic areas, maybe while we have lunch?"

"Anything to get away from the antiseptic smells of this hospital," he stated with a grin. "No offense intended."

Maribel was glad to see his mood lighten up a bit. "No offense taken. I got the idea from one of my professors at U.P. and also from my supervising doctor at the Makati Medical Center in Manila where I also did some intern work. Her experience with patients outside of the hospital setting seemed to make their transition back to normalcy a lot more enjoyable and faster than those patients who were in the hospital during all of their sessions. I'd like to do that too and see if that helps you more as well, if you don't mind."

"Oh, no, not at all. That sounds like a good idea to me. If that helped others recover faster then I'm all for trying that too."

Maribel felt relieved by his positive, even enthusiastic, response. She was also pleased that her patient was smiling again. She thought he looked handsome when he smiled and it made her feel more confident that the counseling session was going well. Self-confidence was an important asset in her line of work.

"Good, good. Well, the fourth thing I want to talk to you about is something we just touched on briefly. Some people feel a need to know why the tragedy that took the life of their loved one occurred. Some people have to rely on the agencies responding to the disaster or event that caused the death of a loved one. As you previously mentioned, you're sure the Viet Cong were the ones responsible for Genevieve's death as well as for the deaths of all the other people on her bus because of the information published in the newspaper article. As to why the bus was blown up, the article described it as a senseless act of terrorism, something the Viet Cong are well known for. How do you feel about that?"

Maribel was not only a good listener but she also watched the faces of her patients for non-verbal signs of communication which was also a form of feedback.

"I think that Genevieve," Ross began in

earnest, with furrowed brows and a serious look on his face, "was the specific target on that bus and all the other passengers were, unfortunately, at the wrong place at the wrong time. In the military, that's known as collateral damage."

Maribel noted his serious look again and asked, "Why do you think that?"

"It's a long story," Ross began, "and it has to do with my wife's father, his business in Saigon and the owner of that business too. It's complicated but I know I'm right about her being singled out and why. Let's move on to another subject, OK?" His tone had become tense and he sounded irritated that someone would doubt him or question his belief.

What he didn't know was, he had been the target of the Viet Cong that day. They had mistakenly thought that Genevieve's uncle, Pierre Ferrand, who sat next to her on the bus, was him. A simple case of mistaken identity had caused his wife, her uncle, thirty other adults, four children and one unborn child to die a horrible death. His wife had only found out the day before her bus trip with her uncle, that she was pregnant. Because she and her uncle were traveling to Vung Tau to bury her father, who had only recently died from a cancerous brain tumor, she had not yet told Ross that he was going to be a father. Had he known all that, all the counseling in the world might not have done him any good.

Maribel again made note of his comments and his demeanor.

"All right," she agreed, "maybe you can tell me about that some other time. The fifth and final thing for today is this: although the healing process may take a long time, you should know that you will heal and recover from this terrible tragedy and your life will continue to have meaning. No one can predict how long you may grieve because we're all different and the circumstances behind each loss of a loved one is different. But, please remember this...it's Doctor Edward's and my job to help you take the necessary steps to ease your progress toward recovery. You're not alone, Tom. Contact either one of us any time you feel the need to talk. Well, that's it for today. Do you have any questions for me?"

"Just one," he said with a pleasant smile on his face, "when is my next appointment?"

CHAPTER 4

The Philippines is a country made up of over 7,000 islands and is located on the Pacific Ocean's Ring of Fire. Some of the volcanoes that are located on the northern island of Luzon are still active, as are some on other islands. Besides the threat of volcanic eruptions, earthquakes are as common in the Philippines as they are in California or Japan.
Since arriving at Clark Air Base, formerly named Clark Field and then Clark Air Force Base, Captain Tom Ross had only experienced one very minor earthquake. He was visiting another member of the OSI detachment he was tentatively assigned to early one evening in the off-base subdivision in Angeles City known as Mountain View.
Captain Ron Chambers had been assigned

as his sponsor, showing him around the base and local areas that included the rows of bars along both sides of an unpaved and very dusty road named Fields Avenue. Captain Chambers, his wife, Debra, and son, Ron, Jr., had been on the waiting list for a house on base for several months and were looking forward to moving out of their rental house in the very near future. The letter from the Base Housing Office, containing an estimated availability date and waiting list number for an on-base house was expected almost any day now.

Ross liked Chambers because of his laid-back way of explaining things like local customs, the martial law situation, and his pleasant personality in general. Chambers was from Wichita, Kansas and didn't mind at all when Ross, from neighboring Oklahoma, showed up at his house wearing jeans with a large Western-style belt buckle and Western-style boots. The Chambers family made Ross feel genuinely welcome into their modest home and he appreciated that a lot. The two men were sitting in the livingroom of the three bedroom stucco house, sipping on cold San Miguels when the windows and doors suddenly began to shake. Soon the whole house was shaking.

Chambers called out to his wife and son and their house girl and then told Ross to follow him to the front door. They all stood there, prepared to go out of the open door if things got much worse. Ross realized that this family had done this before. The shaking lasted less than a minute and didn't cause any damage to the house or any of its contents. It gave them all something new to talk about, as exciting and scary as it was. Because it had been so minor, Ross never gave any thought to earthquakes again. He did, however, think about volcanoes, especially the one he could clearly see from his sponsor's back yard.

Chambers led him out the back door and introduced Ross to Mount Arayat. To the west of Clark Air Base is a long chain of tall mountains, one of which is Mount Pinatubo. To the east, one mountain stood out all alone. Mountain View Subdivision was aptly named because of the unobstructed view one had from there of Mount Arayat, an ancient, dormant volcanoe. Unlike many mountains to the west of Clark Air Base, including Mount Pinatubo, itself another ancient, dormant volcanoe, this one actually looked like a volcanoe, with a tall, pointed cone.

Mount Arayat is in Pampanga Province, in the central part of the island of Luzon. It was off-limits to Americans and Chambers warned Ross about going anywhere near it. A Communist organization called Hukbalahap, or simply "Huks," as Americans called them, made the area on and around Mount Arayat a stronghold and that included a part of nearby Tarlac Province as well.

"Why is it dangerous for Americans to go there?" Ross asked. It looked like it might be a scenic place to visit, especially since anyone at the top could look around 360° in any direction and see the flat countryside far below, for many miles into the distance.

"I've read a couple of books I got at the library," Chambers began, "because I like reading about the history of whatever country I get sent to. This is what I found out and some of it's good and some not-so-good. The Huks helped us fight the Japs here during World War II. When they found out that some Jap soldiers raped some of their women, whenever they came upon a Jap, they cut their heads off with a big sharp bolo. You ever see a bolo?"

"No, not yet. Isn't that some kind of knife, like a big Bowie knife, the kind Jim Bowie invented in the 1830s?"

"Well, it's a knife all right. Only it's twice the size of a Bowie knife, if you can imagine that. They're made of heavy steele with a long single edge, razor sharp and usually have a sturdy wooden handle. So anyway, these Huk Communists killed a lot of Japs in World War II. Just like other guerrilla organizations in the Philippines during the war, we supplied them with guns and ammo to help us fight the Japs. By the end of the war there were around 20,000 armed Huks in the country and between 12,000 to 13,000 of them were on this island, mostly on and around Mount Arayat. They became anti-American and anti-Philippine government as well."

Ross interrupted at this point. "If we supplied them with weapons and ammo to help fight the Japaneses, then why would they be anti-American? That doesn't make any sense to me."

Chambers provided an answer that helped Ross understand their change in heart. "They wanted total independence from any outside influence of foreign countries. They lived under Spanish rule for hundreds of years. Then the U.S. came along and ran things, not granting them independence. After us came the Japanese in 1941 and the Japs treated them badly. When U.S. troops arrived in large numbers and defeated the Japs, the Huks were afraid that we'd stay and run their country again and never leave. They'd had enough of foreign intervention in their country and wanted us to leave after the war. Even though we gave their country independence, the facts remained as they had feared and we never left. We've got bases on Mactan Island near Cebu, Cubi Point Naval

Air Station near Subic Bay Naval Base, Clark Air Base, Camp O'Donnell, Wallace Air Station, Camp John Hay, the JUSMAAG compound in Manila and Marines at the embassy and U.S. military personnel at the airport in Manila as well. Their present government receives millions of dollars in financial aid from our government each year and has agreed to allow this large U.S. military force to remain in their country. That has angered the Huks against their own government, which is pro-American. Does that clear things up for you some?"

Ross nodded, then added, "Yes, quite a bit, thanks."

"And that's not all," Chambers added. "Not only are the Huks a military force, they are a political force too. They want their government to enact land reform programs, to provide better healthcare for the poor, to ensure decent wages for poor farmers of this region of the country and most of all, they want their government to demand the withdrawal of all American military forces and the closing of all our bases. Because the Huks have taken some steps in trying to remedy inequities in their society, they have gained popularity and support from their fellow Philippinos, at least around the Mount Arayat area and Tarlac Province nearby." Jokingly, Chambers ended with, "And that concludes our history lesson for today boys and girls."

Ross laughed along with him and wondered what other things he might learn from Chambers about this place and the current unsettling political situation that caused them to live with a curfew.

"What can you tell me about martial law?"

"What do you want to know about it?"

"Well, for starters," Ross began, "what brought it on? Was there martial law in place when you got here?"

"We got here a couple of months before martial law was declared. What caused it to be declared, according to the Philippine TV news story that was broadcast nation-wide, some anti-government forces, not sure if they were Huks or not, tried to assassinate Philippine Defense Secretary Juan Ponce Enrile. The gunmen failed to hit their target and as many as 20,000 people were arrested during the investigation. President Ferdinand Marcos used that incident as the main reason for declaring martial law on September 22, 1972."

Chambers set his empty beer bottle down on the end table and asked Ross, sitting on the couch next to him, if he was ready for another one. Returning from the kitchen with two cold San Miguels, Chambers quenched his thirst and then continued, but only after a quick question from Ross.

"Is it true that before Marcos was President, he had a private army to protect him in his own province?"

"Let me tell you something," Chambers began, "a lot of the politicians in this country have private armies, not just Marcos, and some of the wealthy businessmen do too. They use their gunmen for their own private security and in some cases, as a means to intimidate their rivals. That's something we OSI agents have to be aware of. We're operating in a very dangerous environment any time we have to leave the base." He looked at Ross to make sure the new man was getting all this.

Ross looked at Chambers when Chambers paused from his talk. "Got it," he said, and Chambers acknowledged him with a nod.

"Back to the martial law thing," Chambers said, wanting to make sure the new guy was fully informed. "When Marcos declared martial law, the 11 p.m. to 5 a.m. curfew went into effect and police checkpoints were set up in many places throughout the country, especially in and around metro Manila. Even the Philippine military was called upon to set up checkpoints. Marcos was quoted in the newspapers and on TV as saying that these steps were necessary to 'provide an atmosphere of peace and order.' He basically used, in basketball terms, a 'full-court press' to lock down the whole country so nobody could oppose him."

"Well, I guess that explains everything," Ross said after taking a long swallow of cold beer from the small brown glass bottle that held the country's number one selling beer.

Rumors went around that formaldehyde, used in embalming fluids to preserve the dead, was also an ingredient used in this popular beer. Some American GIs joked that if you drank too much of the beer and then died, you just made the undertaker's job a little easier. Rumors like this didn't hurt sales of the popular brew one bit.

Chambers then made a statement that really got Ross' attention. "As President of the Philippines, you'd think that Marcos and his family were well-protected and safe from harm, wouldn't you?"

Ross thought about it for a second, then replied, "Well, our president and his family have the Secret Service people protecting them, so yeah, I'd think Marcos had similar protection if not more." He wondered where this was going.

"Nobody in this country is safe from attack, and I mean **nobody**. Back in December 1972, I think it was around the 7th or 8th, anyway, Mrs. Marcos, the Philippine First Lady, was at some kind of public event. A man with a knife got through her security guys and attacked her. Her security detail shot the attacker dead but only after he cut up both of her arms real bad. They rushed her to the hospital and she got both arms stitched up. While she was still in the hospital, Imelda Marcos went on national TV to show everyone that she was still alive. She'd come close to death even when being protected by a presidential security detail. If the attacker had used a gun instead of a knife, she'd probably be dead right now. I'm telling you, this place isn't safe for anyone. That's the environment we're working in now," Chambers stated, with a serious look on his face.

"Wow, I didn't know about all that," Ross replied. "Have any GIs been attacked around here?" he wondered.

"As a matter of fact, I know of one particular case that happened about the time we got here. An Air Force Airman was on a date with a local bar girl at a movie theater downtown. I think it was at night, if I remember correctly. Anyway, someone shot him in the back of the head, killing him instantly. It wasn't a robbery, just a senseless anti-American killing. The person who did it ran out and was never caught," he finished, matter-of-factly.

As if his own personal problems weren't enough to deal with, all the things Ross had heard about while visiting Chambers, specifically all the various dangerous situations in this country, only added more worries. He felt that he'd have to be looking over his shoulders and be extra vigilant whenever he went off base. In some ways, he thought it was almost like being in Vietnam again. Same heat and humidity, same smaller, dark-skinned people who all had brown eyes and dark brown, almost-black hair and most of them walked around in rubber flip-flops, almost like the Ho Chi Minh sandals of Vietnam. The countryside had plenty of coconut trees and rice paddies with water buffalo, or carabao, as they were called here, with young boys riding them or guiding them around. It gave Ross a sense of deja vu, and a bad foreboding feeling as well.

CHAPTER 5

The bangka, a very large canoe-shaped boat with outriggers on both sides for stability in rough seas, rocked gently in the background in fairly shallow water. Four men stood on the sandy beach nearby in stunned silence. Mila, the name of the boat owner's wife, was painted in black on the all-white hull. It was a typical bangka, the Philippino word for boat, one of many boats for hire in this area that took many foreign tourists on fishing or sight-seeing trips. This was one of the most scenic places along the Lingayen Gulf, near Hundred Islands National Park. The South China Sea was only a short distance north of here.

Three of the men standing in the group on the beach had rented the bangka to use as a platform for scuba diving. The fourth man was the bangka's owner-operator. The trio of young Australian tourists had paid for a day that began as a fun-filled summer vacation of scuba diving and spear fishing but was ending up on an ominous note.

This stretch of white sandy beach was in between the coastal town of Lucap and the southern-most of the 123 islands, some of which were no larger than a house, that make up Hundred Islands National Park. It was near here that the tourist's fun turned to fear. A crooked line of small dark clouds glided slowly over the sun-baked sand near Mila and her passengers as the Philippine Constabulary car drove up.

It was late afternoon and still very hot and humid. Cloud formations were building up along the coastline, afternoon rain showers and thunderstorms always a possibility in June. Sergeant Lorenzo Silang parked his vehicle as close to the group of men as he could so he wouldn't have far to walk. The gravel parking lot was empty. He knew that he'd be sweating a lot once he began walking in the hot sand of the beach. The group he was going to talk to, wisely stood in the wet sand at the water's edge.

Sergeant Silang was twenty-nine years old and already a seven year veteran of the PC, Philippine Constabulary, an armed police force organized on military lines but distinct from the regular army. At five-seven, one hundred eighteen pounds, he was of average size compared to the other men in his unit. He called the dispatcher to let them know that he'd arrived at the location he'd been sent to. As soon as he got an acknowledgement, he put his sunglasses on and got out of the patrol car.

It took only a few long strides through the loose, hot sand for Silang to get to within speaking distance of the group of men standing together on the beach. As he got closer, they split into two groups, two going to the left, two going to the right, revealing a big metal object between them. No one spoke a word.

He thought he recognized the oldest man, the Philippino boat owner, wearing an old straw hat that had seen better days. The man was shorter, skinnier, a lot older and much darker than the others. Years at sea and in the sun had darkened and wrinkled his skin considerably. He was the only man with a shirt on too, a dirty old short-sleeved one that had once been white. It had buttons down the front but the man wore it wide open, revealing more dark skin. His shorts looked like an old pair of blue jeans that had been cut off just above the knees and were faded quite a bit by the sun and many years of washing.

The three other men were also barefooted but were wearing swimming trunks of various mixed colors. All three had long, sandy-brown hair, blue eyes and could have been brothers as far as Sergeant Silang was concerned. They looked very fit and trim. If they'd have had military-style haircuts, they could have passed for GIs. Silang guessed they were European tourists.

Hoping that the boat owner/operator could understand some English and maybe the other men as well, he said, "Hello. I am Sergeant Silang from the local Philippine Constabulary office. Did one of you call us?" When he was a kid in school, he'd been required to learn some English and Tagalog, the national dialect of the Philippines. His native dialect was Ilocano, as his family was originally from Vigan, a city on the northwest coast of Luzon, north of here.

In 1762, his great-great-great-great grandfather, Diego Silang, had led an uprising against the ruling Spanish and captured Vigan. His followers named it the capital of Free Ilocos. His heritage was something Sergeant Lorenzo Silang was very proud of.

Before anyone answered, his eyes began to focus on the large metal object that the others had been huddled around only a few moments before. Suddenly, a large dark cloud blocked out the bright sun and Sergeant Silang removed his sunglasses, blinked a few times, and then refocused his eyes. He'd seen old 55-gallon drums before at some gas stations and boat docks but this one was somehow different. It was full of holes, and, upon closer examination, looked like dozens of bullet holes.

The Philippino with the straw hat stepped forward and introduced himself as Gregorio Arroyo, owner of the nearby boat. He'd spent his entire adult life at sea. He looked older than fifty-seven, with crow's feet and other lines creasing his weathered, clean-shaven face. His straw hat covered most of his white hair, which his wife kept neatly trimmed for him. Men tended to gray early in his family. Now his hair was beyond gray, looking almost as white as his thin cotton shirt. A few inches shorter than Sergeant Silang and a lot thinner, he stood out in stark contrast next to the trio of younger men he was with.

He pointed in the direction of the other men in swimming trunks and said, "These men hired me to take them diving and spear fishing. After that, I was going to take them over to Quezon and Marcos Islands in the Hundred Islands National Park, to do a little sight-seeing. Just as they were about to return to the boat after they finished scuba diving, they discovered this steel drum with a body in it. I was the one who called the police from the restaurant just down the road."

Sergeant Silang nodded his head in acknowledgement of the old man's story. The dispatcher had told him that a steel drum with a body inside had been reported, so he was mentally prepared for that, but still... inside of a steel drum full of bullet holes, and at the bottom of the sea? That was a new experience for him, as he was sure it was for these men as well.

"Did you look inside the drum?" Sergeant Silang asked, after a long pause.

"Yes, I opened it after those guys got it up on the boat. It's not every day that somebody finds a 55-gallon drum full of holes at the bottom of the sea, you know? We were all curious, so I opened it." Having said that, Gregorio stood there with his arms crossed, then asked, "What would you have done?"

"Probably the same thing," Sergeant Silang replied. He took a couple of steps and then looked down into the drum. The top was laying next to it in the sand. The heat and humidity caused him to start sweating and it didn't take long for big wet spots to appear on his uniform shirt. He wiped a bead of sweat from his brow with his right hand while leaning over to take a closer look.

He made the mistake of breathing normally as he got his head to within a few inches of the top of the head of the body that was in the barrel that once contained oil. The putrid stench was overpowering and he reeled back, retching and dry-heaving as he fell to his knees in the warm sand.

None of the others had ventured to get that close to the body once the top of the steel cylinder had been removed. The terrible odor of the decomposing corpse stayed within the drum for the most part and could not be detected at all from a couple of feet away.

    Sergeant Silang took a moment to recover, stood back up, and then spoke his mind.

    "I don't know who he was or what he did but somebody was sure pissed off at him. Looks like they stuffed him in there and then had target practice with a machine gun or something. That poor guy is tore up bad." With a look of pity on his face, he shook his head back and forth. "That's a helluva way to die." Then he reached into his back pocket and took out a red bandana and wiped his face and neck. He was feeling the effects of the heat and humidity even more now.

    Sergeant Silang held the bandana over his nose and mouth and went back for another look. From where he stood, he could see that the body took up most of the space in the tightly-packed steel cylinder. Due to the way it was wedged in, very little could be seen below the shoulders. It was a real mess from the shoulders up. He thought it was a man because of the short hair but couldn't begin to guess the victim's age.

    He shuddered and stepped back again, turning away from the grisly scene. He then folded up the bandana and put it back in his pocket while sucking in lungs full of clean, fresh air in several deep breaths. Whoever this was, he thought, did, indeed, die a horrible death.

    The sun came out from behind the clouds and the beach suddenly became much brighter. Sergeant Silang quickly put his silver-rimmed sunglasses back on. He was getting hot and thirsty and thought the other men probably felt the same way. He knew it was time to press on. The three men in swimming trunks were shifting their weight from one foot to the other. They probably wanted to get out of the direct sunlight too, as well as away from the stinking corpse in the steel drum.

"Who all knows about this?" Sergeant Silang asked the boat owner.

"Only us here and the person at the police station who answered the phone and you," replied the old man.

Sergeant Silang reached down and picked up the round metal top to the drum and set it lightly in place to keep the body covered up. He then turned and faced the men still standing quietly nearby. They had all congregated back into one group, several feet away from, and upwind of the steel drum, waves of warm salt water washing up to their feet. Except for the boat owner/operator, none of the tourists had spoken a single word so far.

"I've got to report this to my commander. It may take a while for him to get here, so if you all want to find some shade somewhere or make a call to let someone know you'll be here for some time, go ahead. It's OK to go back on the boat as well, just don't take it anywhere. Mr. Arroyo, I appreciate your help. I'll be back as soon as I can." With that said, he turned and strode through the loose sand as quickly as he could, back to his patrol car. Once there, he had to empty some sand out of his shoes.

As he was sitting in the car with the door open, putting his shoes back on, the young man wearing bright green swimming trunks walked up to him.

"Excuse me, sir," the barefoot man said, with a distinctively Aussie accent, "I'm Allan Wingate. My friends and I are on vacation. We have to start back to Manila tomorrow morning to catch our plane home and we were wondering if we're going to be delayed from doing that."

Sergeant Silang looked up at the young

man from his driver's seat and kept his reply short. "You will probably get to leave on time. We just need some information from each of you about what you saw today and where we can reach you if we have any more questions. We will get your written statements when I return with my commander. He handles all the paperwork."

"OK then, thank you." He almost added "mate" out of habit but caught himself at the last second, deciding it best not to.

As soon as the young man turned to leave, Sergeant Silang started the engine to the Philippine Constabulary patrol car and turned up the air conditioner full-blast. He felt bad for the foreign vacationers. Tourists brought lots of money into the local economy. He hoped this incident wouldn't cause any of them to stay away from this area in the future. He didn't doubt that the three men would probably talk about this when they got back home to Australia. Word about the killing would surely spread. And what of that poor soul in the old oil barrel? Who knows what might happen when news gets out about that around here.

Four men sat together at a table in the back corner of a Chinese restaurant. It was located on MacArthur Highway in Angeles City, about a mile from the main gate of Clark Air Base. Bhoy Santos sat on one side of the table with Rico Salazar at the narrow end and two other hired hands, Edwin Sanchez and Carlos Reyes sitting across from Santos. Two of the six armed men who had driven here from Manila with Bhoy Santos were at a nearby table. One man stayed outside in their jeepney to keep it from being stolen. Jeepney thefts had been on the rise lately.

This particular restaurant was one of their favorite places to conduct business because of the location, good food and cold beer. The aroma of food being cooked in giant woks in the kitchen, the clinking sounds of dinnerware and silverware and low volume, friendly conversations of many diners nearby made it an environment that Bhoy Santos felt comfortable in. It reminded him of his grandmother's house during festive family get-togethers when he was a young boy.

"Well, Rico, how did your trip to Hundred Islands go?" Bhoy Santos smiled up at the young waitress after asking the question, telling her to come back in about five minutes. His friendly smile helped him set people at ease and he used that often, to his advantage. Looking at him, one would never imagine that he was a cold-blooded killer.

Rico replied, "No problems, Mr. Santos. We did just as you instructed. The man you said was an OSI agent would not admit to anything. He kept insisting that he was minding his own business, not investigating drug deals at all. He claimed to be just a regular GI to the very end."

Rico Salazar was one of Bhoy Santos' hired thugs. He was a twenty-nine year old elementary school drop-out. He was big and mean and had been in trouble with the law several times. His five-ten, one hundred seventy pound frame was very tanned and muscular due to fifteen years of working as a logger in the mountains of northern Luzon. He was a lot larger than the average size Philippino and that was one of the reasons Bhoy Santos hired him as a "handy man."

"I would have said the same thing if I was him," Edwin piped in. "Wouldn't you, Carlos?"

Edwin Sanchez was a long-time friend of

Rico Salazar. They'd met years ago when they both worked for the same logging company. He was also twenty-nine years old. He stood just five-eight but a beer gut, caused by a love of beer, brought his weight up to a whopping two hundred pounds, really heavy for a Philippino. Like his friend Rico, Edwin was a match for anyone in a fight, which is why he too had had a few run-ins with the police.

"You are right about that, my friend!" Carlos replied, with a big toothy grin.

All three "handy men" nodded an affirmative, heads bobbing up and down in unison. Carlos Reyes was the youngest, shortest and lightest of the men sitting at the table. At twenty-five, he was also the only one married. He was a master auto mechanic and auto thief and didn't mind lending a hand and earning extra money when his friends Rico and Edwin came calling. He'd met them a couple of years ago when he was called upon to fix one of their broken-down logging trucks.

Bhoy Santos grinned at Carlos' reply and nodded his approval. Looking directly at Rico, he asked, "Did you try to persuade him to talk?" A lot of emphasis had been placed on the word **persuade**.

Rico, the spokesman for the three men sitting at the table with Santos, replied, "Yes, Mr. Santos, one finger at a time. After losing a couple, he yelled that we were making a big mistake."

"My sources do not make such mistakes. If they said the guy was American OSI, then that's what he was. How did you finally get rid of him?"

"We took him to the Lingayen Gulf near Hundred Islands National Park on a fishing trip. I made sure he couldn't tell where he was. We tied his wrists and ankles with duct tape and put a dark hood over his head the whole time, until we got out into deep water, far from shore. We put him into a 55-gallon drum and then took the hood off and the tape off of his mouth. I told him that he had one last chance to tell us why he was snooping around."

Santos was enjoying the story. He smiled at this and then asked, "What did he say to that?"

"He said, and I quote, 'Go to hell!' So out in the Lingayen Gulf, with nobody around to hear it, Edwin gave him a 21-gun salute, not once, but twice, and a watery burial at sea." He knew that Mr. Santos appreciated his morbid sense of humor.

Their boss chuckled as he imagined the scene just described to him, then said, "Nagugutom po ako. Handa na po akong mag-order," (I'm hungry. I'm ready to order) and waved a waitress over to their table.

Since he was paying for everyone's meal, he ordered his favorite things for them all: ice cold San Miguel beer, chicken fried rice, pork adobo, pancit and pork lumpia.

Discussing a murder at the dinner table was no big deal to Bhoy Santos and his gang. To them, it was just another day at the office. The question no one asked was, who would be their next victim? They knew it was only a matter of time.

CHAPTER 6

"How are you feeling today?" Maribel Edwards asked. She couldn't help but notice the man sitting across from her was looking sharper and happier than he'd been at his last appointment. Ross' recent haircut made his hair appear a shade lighter, especially around his temples and that, combined with the grin on his face, gave him a younger appearance. He was definitely a good looking man, she thought.
"You don't stop being a woman just because you start being a doctor," one of her female mentors at the Makati Medical Center had once told her. That simple statement resonated with her.
"Pretty good. I can't complain," he replied, then took another sip of ice tea.
This counseling session was being held outside on a covered patio behind the 13th

Air Force Regional Medical Center. They sat on opposite sides of a small white table with their ice teas and ham and cheese sandwiches. To Ross, it was a much more relaxed atmosphere here than the inside of Maribel's small office. He liked her idea of holding sessions outside of the hospital. He liked it a lot and it showed.

Besides her lunch, Maribel had a notepad and pen on the table. After finishing their lunch, she got right to the point. Even though there were other people eating their lunches at nearby tables, everyone would be too involved in their own conversations to pay any attention to what she had to say.

"As far as your grief counseling goes, I've only got a few more things to cover. Then we'll start on your psychoanalysis, OK?"

"Yeah, and thanks for inviting me out here. Except for the flies and humidity, it's a nicer, more laid-back environment, better than your office for sure."

"Yes, that's definitely true," she agreed. Then she began with the next topic on the counseling agenda. "Believe it or not, Tom, the emotional stress of dealing with death can supress your body's immune system, making you more susceptible to illness. To counteract that possibility, let me suggest a few things, OK?"

"OK."

The brightness of the natural light outdoors, even in the shade, provided Ross with a different look at Maribel's features. He noticed how more slightly rounded and wider her nose seemed to be, compared to when he saw her under the fluorescent lights of the hospital. That, and the ever-so-slight, almond shape of her brown eyes, gave her that half-Asian, half-European look that had captivated his imagination when he'd met

Genevieve for the first time on that sidewalk in Saigon. He wondered if Maribel was also part Asian. Either way, he felt that she was not quite as pretty as Genevieve, but still very attractive nonetheless.

"You should try and get plenty of sleep and try to maintain a regular sleep schedule as much as possible. Am I boring you, Tom?" she asked, sounding a bit irritated. She noticed that he looked as if he wasn't paying any attention at all, daydreaming perhaps.

"Oh, no. I just...well, I guess my mind drifted off for some reason. Sorry," he said, with an embarrassed look on his face. "Please continue."

She didn't know that he'd been comparing her looks to that of his deceased wife. She glared at him like a teacher who'd just caught a student doing something he should not have been doing in class and only after a long silent pause, continued.

"In addition to getting enough sleep, you should also avoid any kind of drugs or alcohol that may be used in an attempt to lessen any emotional pain you may find yourself experiencing. You can get a perscription from Doctor Edwards for medication for any sleeplessness, intense emotional, or other physical problems you may have, now or in the future."

Maribel paused to take a sip of her ice tea and noticed that Ross seemed to be paying more attention now.

"Another thing that may help you," she continued, "is regular exercise, at least some type of exercise for half an hour each day, even if it's just walking fast. Also, you should try and eat regular nutritious meals too," she added.

"You mean like the ham and cheese sandwiches we just ate?" he asked, sarcastically.

He grinned at her, hoping she had a good sense of humor.

"Your sarcasm means you've been paying attention," she stated with a big smile, once again reminding him of his wife. They both had perfect teeth that were revealed when they smiled. "It was a pretty good sandwich though, wasn't it?"

He had to agree with her on that point. "Yeah, it was at that. Better than I had expected in fact. This ice tea is pretty good too," he added, taking another sip and enjoying the cold refreshment that helped him stay cool on this warm, humid day.

"The next thing I'd like to address are your emotional needs. One of the key things essential to recovery from the death of a loved one is, not to let go of the one who died, but of your need for them. Do you understand what I mean by that?" Maribel was hoping for a positive answer.

Ross hesitated before answering, literally repeating those words in his mind, "not to let go of the one who died, but of your need for them."

"Yes, I think I understand what that means." He wasn't sure if he could do it, but he understood what she meant. The memories of intimate times with Genevieve were still fresh, as if it was only yesterday and he sometimes felt the need for more. Wasn't that a normal human feeling? How could he let go of that? According to what he was being told now, he had to.

Maribel was happy at not having to dwell on this particular subject, possibly having to explain with the use of examples, and so she pressed on. "As I mentioned before, the grieving process and recovery is just that, a process. It's important that you talk and share your feelings about your wife with your family and friends."

Before she could say another word, he interrupted her with, "My family and friends are back in the States, in Oklahoma."

She was quick with a reply. "Then maybe you should take some time off, perhaps a week or two of leave time and fly back to Oklahoma and spend some time with your family and friends there."

"I'll think about it," he replied, not really looking forward to a tearful reunion with his parents, who had not been given the opportunity to meet their daughter-in-law in person.

"You could also keep a journal and write about your emotions. You can keep track of your progress that way too," she suggested.

He didn't reply to that idea, only shaking his head in acknowledgement. He'd never been the type of person to keep any kind of journal or diary and he wasn't about to start now just because she had suggested it. That's not for me, he thought.

"You could also pass the time, when you aren't working, by doing things you enjoy, like reading a book, watching a movie, or working out at the gym."

Maribel paused for another refreshing sip of cold ice tea but by now most of the ice had melted and it diluted the flavor quite a bit. She watched her patient's face for any signs of acknowledgement, agreement, understanding, anything that would give her a clue about how she was doing as his grief counselor. Only time would tell, she told herself. She didn't notice anything just now that revealed much of anything in his eyes or face in regards to a reaction. She remembered what her father called that look, a "poker face."

"Do you have any questions so far, Tom?"

"No, not yet anyway. Maybe later." He took another sip of his drink, now mostly water from the melted ice. At least it was cold.

She nodded in reply to his answer and then continued on. "You're going to have some difficult times ahead during those special days like your wife's birthday or your wedding anniversary. You may want to find ways to change those traditions while still honoring your wife's memory."

Maribel knew this information by heart but wished she could have done a better job with her delivery. She was her own harshest critic. Dealing with a real patient instead of practicing on a classmate wasn't the same thing and she knew that more experience was what she needed.

His reply to that information surprised her, but in a good way. It was a positive sign that he was making progress. "Maribel, Genevieve and I were together for less than a year and so there was only her one birthday together. We had not been married long enough for an anniversary. That's why I don't think any specific dates will cause me any problems to have to deal with," he stated matter-of-factly.

She nodded in understanding and brushed some hair back from the side of her face after a short-lived breeze blew it there. Maribel then summed up the information that she'd given Ross during the session with him so far. Just like one of her college professors had taught her at U.P.: "Tell them what you're going to tell them, then tell them, then tell them what you told them." Her time with him as a grief counselor was coming to an end, unless he asked her for help. The only thing left now were the sessions of psychoanalysis.

"Tom, that's all the information I have for you right now. Just remember that Doctor Edwards and I are here to help you any time you need us. Please don't hesitate to ask for help. It may take a while for the grieving process to be over and nobody can predict how long because each case is different. Just try to determine which things work best for you and be patient. In time, you'll get through this. You may not feel that way now, but it will happen. Remember, talking about it always helps, so you can call me any time you want to talk. Oh yeah, before I forget, I wrote down on this piece of paper the date and time of your first psychoanalysis session, along with my phone number."

She handed him the piece of paper and told him, "It's next Tuesday at 9 a.m. Wear some civilian clothes, something casual. We'll be having our sessions at different places each week, away from the hospital, in a relaxing environment. Do you have any questions for me?" she asked, as she began rising from her chair.

"I finally thought of one," he said, also rising from the table they'd been sitting at for the last hour. "Are you related to Doctor Edwards? You two have the same last name and I was just wondering."

Maribel picked up her note pad, pen and empty drink cup and replied with a broad smile, proudly proclaiming, "Yes, as a matter of fact, Doctor Edwards is my father. And in case you were wondering about something else, my mother was born and raised in the Philippines, so I'm half-American and half-Philippino." Then she turned away and walked back into the hospital, headed for her father's office to give him a patient update on Captain Tom Ross.

"Well, I'll be doggone," Ross muttered to himself as he watched Maribel walk away.

Now, for the second time in his life, in two different countries, he'd met two attractive half-Asian, half-Caucasian women and their Caucasian fathers.  He'd heard of the phrase, "history repeating itself," before, but this new revelation was just so bizarre, he didn't know what to make of it.

"I'll be doggone," he repeated, as he tossed his empty drink cup into a nearby trash can.  He left the hospital grounds thinking only about this incredible coincidence and wondered if it would be followed by any other coincidences in the future. Only time would tell, he told himself.  Only time would tell.

## CHAPTER 7

The telephone rang. Then it rang again. Finally, Major Dickinson answered it. He was the Air Force Office of Special Investigations detachment commander at Clark Air Base. It was a busier than normal day at the small OSI office. The phone had been ringing off the hook and Fred Dickinson was about ready for another aspirin. His wife had called earlier in the day to talk to him about how they would celebrate his birthday coming up later in the week when he would turn "the Big Four-O" as she put it. He wanted to take her and their ten year old son, Jake, horseback riding and have a cook-out under one of the picnic pavilians over by the riding stables. She wanted just the two of them to go out with some friends to the O-Club, to wine, dine and dance. That was aspirin number one.

"No wonder my hair is starting to turn gray," he mumbled to himself. He recognized the voice on the phone immediately. "Hi, Dave! What's new?"

Dave Stoneman was one of his fellow ROTC cadets from their Valdosta State University days. They'd stayed in touch over the years and both of them had been assigned to the Philippines, although at different locations. Dave was now the commander of the security police detachment at Wallace Air Station. It was located on Poro Point, near the city of San Fernando in La Union Province, several hours drive north of Clark Air Base. The South China Sea was on three sides of Wallace Air Station, making for some beautiful scenic views, especially with steep cliffs, a lighthouse, and a private beach nearby.

"I've got some bad news, Fred. Really bad. Some Australian tourists were scuba diving near Hundred Islands National Park southwest of here a few days ago. They discovered a 55-gallon drum with a badly shot-up body inside." Dave paused to look down at the paper on his desk with the information on it. "The Philippine Constabulary took the body to their forensics people in Baguio. There were many bullet holes in both the drum and the body. They contacted me after checking to see if the victim was stationed at Camp John Hay in Baguio. He wasn't stationed here either and so I decided to see if maybe he was one of your guys."

Dickinson groaned and an "Oh no," barely audible over the phone lines, slipped out.

"What did you say, Fred?"

"What's the guy's name, Dave?"

"I was told his name is Travis B. Davis. Is he one of yours?" For the sake of his friend, Dave hoped the victim was from another unit.

Dickinson knew everyone in his detachment and didn't need to consult a personnel roster. Travis B. Davis was one of his agents, a single First Lieutenant. Damn!

"Unfortunately Dave, yes, he's one of my agents. Apparently his cover must have been blown somehow. I can't tell you anything about the case he was working on over this unsecured line. Can you assist in getting his remains back here?"

"My counterpart at Camp John Hay will have his remains on a chopper to Clark as soon as the ink drys on the paperwork, transferring custody of the remains from the Philippine Constabulary to American authorities. I was told there will be a joint PC/American investigation as this is being treated as a homicide at the international level. I'm really sorry, Fred."

"Thanks, Dave. I'll be in touch."

The already thinly-spread AFOSI detachment at Clark Air Base was now down a man. A good man too, according to his commander. But how had his cover been blown? Major Dickinson agonized over the loss and was now faced with a tough decision. Who could he replace Lieutenant Davis with? The drug investigation he'd been working on had to be continued. Too many GIs in various locations in the Philippines had been using drugs. They had to find the sources, and soon.

There was talk of a new program that would replace the old one. The Drug Rehabilitation Program, which helped GIs quit their drug habit without discharging them from the military, was going to be replaced by a "zero tolerance" program. Since the withdrawal of U.S. troops from Vietnam and another big down-sizing of total military forces, which included the end of the draft, one way to lower the numbers of military personnel was to discharge anyone found using drugs. Urinalysis testing was in full-swing now and the days of drug rehab were numbered.

It might take several weeks or even a month or two before a replacement for Davis would arrive from the States. This investigation needed to be pursued ASAP, especially in light of what just happened. Davis must have been on to something important. Otherwise why would anyone kill him? These thoughts went through Dickinson's mind as he eventually came to the realization that there was only one person not currently assigned to a case, and that person was Captain Tom Ross.

While Ross was only tentatively assigned to the unit, pending the final outcome of his psychological evaluation, he'd been given the duty of assisting the Merchandise Control Office. Day in and day out, he had the job of screening the purchase records of individuals in the military and their dependants for any signs of black marketing. That literally included the thousands of personnel assigned here. It was tedious, boring work but Major Dickinson felt that Ross had to do something worthwhile to occupy his time when not at a medical appointment.

Dickinson called Doctor Edwards and discussed Ross' progress and the need to return him to the field where his experience as an investigator could be best utilized. His training and expertise were being wasted at Merchandise Control. The doctor told him he needed to speak with another counselor first, before he could give his final answer and would call him back later in the day.

"Maribel, how's your patient progressing? I got a call from his commander today, wanting to know if he can be returned to unrestricted duty again."

Maribel Edwards had brought her patient's medical records and her notes with her to her father's office. They were alone now and could speak more freely, unlike their business-like conversations when around the hospital staff.

"He's making very good progress, Dad, but there's still more work to be done as far as his treatment goes."

She was about to say more but her father cut her off. "Would it be possible, given his good progress, that the rest of his counseling sessions could be cut a little short by out-patient treatment, say, you meeting with him at other locations outside of the hospital?"

"I'm already doing that to some extent. He seems to open up more and feels more at ease to talk about himself when we're outdoors, like on the back patio break area. I've planned on trying other locations like the riding stables picnic area or maybe even some off-base locations. Would that be all right?"

"You're a chip off the old block, as they say. Absolutely! If getting away from here speeds up his recovery, by all means, take as many 'field trips' as I like to call them as necessary. But, please be very careful. Some places off base can still be dangerous, even under martial law, especially for Americans. You could be mistaken for an American too you know, at least from a distance." He thought his daughter favored her mother a lot and looked more Philippino than American. "You can blame me for that!" He laughed a little and then finished with, "And don't forget the curfew hours off base too. You know me, no matter how old you are, you're still my daughter and I'll always worry about your well-being."

He reached across the desk and caressed Maribel's cheek with the back of his right hand, looking her in the eyes.

"You've made me so very proud. I have every confidence in you to help your patient return to his old self again and get over his loss, just like we had to get over our loss when your mother died." A father's pride showed on his beaming face as he stood up and walked around his desk and gave his daughter a hug. "I love you. Never forget that. Now, get out of here before I get all emotional and teary-eyed," he said as he kissed her on the cheek.

She hugged him back and said, "I love you too, Dad. I'll continue to keep you posted."

She didn't want to leave his office looking like she'd been emotional either. It wasn't easy to maintain a professional relationship at all times with her father, not saying "Dad" instead of "Doctor Edwards" and having to put on a straight face and speak in a formal tone when others were around. Still, she'd rather finish her internship here than anywhere else.

After getting the return call from Doctor Edwards, Major Dickinson called Ross in for a quick meeting.

"Tom, I've got some good news and some bad. First, the good news. I'm taking you off of Merchandise Control duty." He saw an immediate reaction in Ross' face when he made that announcement and it was a good one that began with a big smile.

"Good! I'm tired of looking at how many cartons of cigarettes or bottles of liquor that Sergeant So-And-So and his wife bought last month. Talk about boring work!" he stated, with much relief.

"Boring, yet necessary," came the reply. "Too many people have taken advantage of buying duty-free and tax-free goods on base and then selling the stuff on the black market off base for huge profits. Almost half of our case load involves black marketing activities. Now for the bad news. I know you didn't get to meet First Lieutenant Travis Davis because he was out on an assignment when you got here. Well, he was working on a case involving American airmen at different locations. He was trying to find the source of the drugs they were caught with. Unfortunately, he's dead now." He paused a moment to take a sip of his still-cold soda he'd picked up on his lunch break. He peered intently at Ross to guage his reaction.

"How did he die?" Ross showed no reaction to the news of the lieutenant's death so far.

"I was told that some Australian tourists were scuba diving up north of here, near Hundred Islands National Park in the Lingayen Gulf. They came across a 55-gallon drum that was full of bullet holes. Davis' body had been stuffed inside and he was shot up pretty bad. The Philippine Constabulary were called and they checked to see if Davis was assigned to either Camp John Hay in Baguio or Wallace Air Station north of Hundred Islands once they found his ID card and discovered that he was an American serviceman. Those are the two closest bases we have to where he was found. A friend of mine at Wallace gave me the news. They tortured Davis before murdering him too."

"How do they know he was tortured?"

"Davis was missing some fingers and the forensics people are sure they were cut off and not shot off when his killers used him for target practice," he replied bitterly.

"Damn!" was all Ross could say, shaking his head, a grimace and look of disbelief on his face.

"The bad news doesn't end there either.

Headquarters doesn't have anyone in the pipeline to replace Davis and the case he was working on is too important to either shit-can it or put it on the back burner. We've got to make do with what we've got. Your clearance to work here was contingent upon your mental state of mind as determined by Doctor Edwards and my final say-so. I don't have anyone else available to take over Davis' case. If I did, believe me, we wouldn't be having this conversation," the major stated emphatically.

A mental image of a man stuffed into a 55-gallon drum with some fingers cut off, shot full of holes and dropped into the ocean, was occupying Ross' mind when a dead silence finally snapped him back to Major Dickinson. The major was intently staring at him. Not good.

"Are you listening to me, Tom? You've got that 'thousand yard stare,' again," Dickinson said, wondering if Ross was mentally ready for duty again. He'd heard of that type of look that was seen in the faces of men returning from duty in Vietnam. He was aware that some of them had witnessed and experienced some terrible things over there that would torment their minds for the rest of their lives. Was Ross one of them?

"Yes, sir. Sorry 'bout that. I was just thinking about what you said in regards to Davis having been tortured before he was killed. That's pretty gruesome if you ask me."

"You're damn right it is!" He took in, then let out, a very long breath. "After consulting with your doctor, I've decided to turn Davis' case over to you, but only if you tell me, in no uncertain terms, that you're ready for this. And one more thing. You're to continue meeting with your grief counselor," not remembering what other term to use for Ross' psychiatrist at the moment, "until I hear from Doctor Edwards that you are one hundred percent finished with all of your appointments. I think you've still got a few more sessions, right?"

"Yes, sir, that's right. I feel up to the task. I think getting back to work in my regular line of investigating will do me a lot of good," Ross stated sincerely.

"All right then. Davis had his assignment folder filed under his name in the file cabinet right across from my office. Read over everything thoroughly and don't hesitate to ask me or anyone else here for help. Draw a weapon from the armory in the small building out behind this one and schedule yourself some time on the firing range. Come back the day after tomorrow and your blanket travel orders, ration card and other things will be ready to pick up. Any questions?"

"What about transportation?" he wondered, "for traveling from base to base."

"See Sergeant St. Claire in the orderly room. He'll tell you what you need to know about that. If you had a government license in Vietnam, then you'll just have to get it stamped with 'CLARK AIR BASE' on it over at the base motor pool. Anything else?"

"No, sir. See you the day after tomorrow then."

Ross felt so relieved that he didn't have to report to the Merchandise Control Office any more. However, it was just now starting to sink in as to the gravity of the situation. Taking over an investigation that got his predecessor not only killed, but horribly tortured and then killed. This is some serious shit, he thought, as he left the AFOSI building and headed for the armory to get a gun.

CHAPTER 8

    The meeting between Bhoy Santos and Mang Binh Hao had gone well. The weather had been sunny and warm and the seas remained calm during the entire trip from Saigon to Manila. The Lady of the Seas was berthed at pier five in North Harbor.
    Shortly after Customs cleared the ship and crew, the unloading of millions of dollars worth of opium, heroin and marijuana began. By that time it was late in the afternoon. Most of the drugs were hidden inside of large ceramic elephants that were hollow inside. Measuring about eighteen inches tall, twelve inches wide and sixteen inches long, the elephants had a flat surface on their backs for placing potted plants.
    Beautifully hand-painted to resemble elephants wearing a harness that held a flat

cargo-carrying platform on their backs, with large colorful blankets between their hides and the platform, the ceramic pieces were in straw-cushioned crates marked 'GULF OF LION SHIPPING CO.' in large black letters. They had shipping documents folded inside of a plastic pouch stapled to the outside of each wooden crate. It was an ingenious disguise which allowed the innocent-looking merchandise to be shipped almost anywhere.

To avoid the scrutiny of the guards who patrolled the harbor area or the police, who manned highway checkpoints, Bhoy Santos used a dozen jeepneys instead of one large truck to transport the drug-laden crates to different destinations. On top of the wooden crates, he had his men place baskets of fruit and vegetables, as if they were poor farmers taking their produce to market. The "Trojan horse" technique, employed by both Mang Binh Hao and his Philippine connection, Bhoy Santos, worked every time and the flow of drugs to each dealer throughout the country never slowed down.

Occasionally, Santos would send some drugs to Cebu to a man who had a small operation of his own, selling mostly marijuana to American servicemen stationed at Mactan Air Base on nearby Mactan Island. Remy Minaguet owned a small tire repair shop a few blocks northeast of Fort San Pedro, on a side street that dead-ends at South Osmeña Boulevard to the northwest and Quezon Boulevard to the southeast. His tire repair business made enough money to support a wife and four kids but thirty-two year old Remy had a girlfriend on the side. That's why he decided to get involved in the drug business as a means of making money his wife would not know about.

*********************************************

At the conclusion of one of his appointments, Maribel invited Ross to travel with her and her father to Cebu. That was where she was born and where her mother was buried. Her mother had died five years ago from cervical cancer. Maribel and her father traveled back to Cebu each year on the anniversary of her mother's death to place some fresh flowers on her grave and pay their respects. At the last moment, something had come up and Doctor Edwards couldn't go but urged Maribel and Ross to go without him.

Ross had just received a new case to work on but didn't have to start until Monday. He was free to take the weekend off and go to Cebu with Maribel. He didn't know when or even if he'd ever get the chance to go there again and so he decided it was "now or never." Maribel told him that his psychoanalysis sessions could be done on the trip and not just at the Clark Air Base hospital. That fact made the trip even more appealing to him.

The cargo hold of the U.S. Air Force C-130 Hercules was very noisy so whenever they talked to one another, Ross and Maribel had to lean up against eachother and speak directly into one another's ears. They were buckled in next to eachother, sitting only a few feet away from the front troop door on red, side-facing canvas seats that were held in place by an aluminum frame. There were eight Space-Available passengers aboard with them, along with several pallets of netted cargo, all manifested from Clark to Mactan Air Base.

"You said that you and your father make this same trip each year?" Ross almost yelled in order to be heard.

Shaking her head, Maribel replied, leaning to her left, up against Ross, "Yes. We visit my mother's grave on the anniversary of her death." She kept her answer short because of the noisy interior of the four-engined plane and also because she wasn't used to having to raise her normally soft voice so much in order to be heard. She wondered why Ross had asked that question. After all, she'd explained the reason for the trip at the hospital only a few days ago.

"I'll wait 'til we get off the plane before I ask any more questions, OK?" Ross shouted in her ear, loud enough to make her wince from the volume.

Maribel only nodded in reply. They had both been offered a set of small rubber earplugs by the aircraft loadmaster but neither of them had used them yet. They would soon though and then they both nodded off a few minutes afterwards because of the early Space-A call for this flight that was made at the MAC terminal at 0545 that morning. Neither Maribel nor Ross had slept much the night before.

As in Vietnam, Ross was authorized to work and travel in civilian clothes. His travel orders allowed him to transit between military bases using any form of transportation available, with a military travel status of a TDY, temporary duty. Maribel, on the other hand, had to sign up in the Space-A book at the passenger terminal at Clark, traveling on a space-available basis. She also had to show her American passport and visa. For both, it was a free roundtrip plane ride.

She'd made this same journey several times before with her father. That's why she was prepared for the cold temperature in the plane. She wore white tennis shoes with white socks, form-fitting, tailor-made blue jeans she had made for her at a local

Angeles City tailor shop, a powder blue blouse and a light blue sweater. Light blue was her favorite color.

Ross was the only passenger on the plane that looked like he was headed for a rodeo. He wore tan Western-style boots, the type some people referred to as "cowboy" boots. To him, they were just ordinary work boots, not the fancy, hand-tooled, leather, dressy kind some men wore with their Sunday suits. His blue jeans were starting to fade from their original darker tint and were held in place by his favorite wide, tan, leather belt that was a perfect match with his boots. Adorning the front of the belt was a large, silver buckle with the letters "TR" engraved in it. His parents had given that to him as a birthday gift several years ago. He didn't like to wear ball caps or hats of any kind when wearing "civvies." His medium gray pull-over polo shirt, with a couple of buttons and a collar, was covered up with a windbreaker-type light jacket, also a medium gray in color. Whenever he noticed someone looking down their nose at him for the way he dressed, he always thought the same thing, no matter where he was at the time. I'm from Oklahoma by God and if you don't like the way I dress, well, that's just too damn bad!

As their plane flew at high altitude across the blue morning sky in a southeasterly direction, crossing the Sibuyan Sea and nearing the island of Masbate, north of the island of Cebu, the plane banked slightly, causing Maribel's head to roll to the left. It ended up against Ross' upper right arm. The earplugs she had eventually inserted, helped her to finally fall into a deep sleep. Her father had once told her that, as a kid, she would fall asleep easily on any trip, whether they were on a plane, train or bus. That had not changed one bit as she grew older.

Ross had also used the earplugs he'd been given and he too was sound asleep. When Maribel's head pressed up against his right arm just below his shoulder, he instinctively put his arm around her and pulled her close. That's what he'd always done whenever Genevieve did that. It just came naturally, without a thought.

When the aircraft loadmaster went around waking everyone up because they were about to land, Ross gently removed his arm from around Maribel, wondering how it had gotten there in the first place. He had no memory of doing that and was wondering what the consequences might be. He was mentally preparing himself to make an apology and, at the same time, hoping it wouldn't become necessary. He was dreading what Maribel's first words to him might be. What the hell have I done, he wondered to himself.

Maribel blinked her eyes a few times and yawned as soon as she began waking up to the voice of the loadmaster. She barely noticed the slight movement across her shoulders as Ross gingerly removed his right arm. When she turned to look at him, the first thing that entered her mind was, he's got that "hand caught in the cookie jar" look.

"I'm sorry," he began, "I was just stretching my arms after I woke up and did not realize I was so close to hitting you in the head. Are you OK?" He hoped she would believe that. He was too embarrassed to admit the truth, that in his sleep, he may have thought she was Genevieve.

"Yes, I'm fine. No need to apologize. It's no big deal, really," she said with a reassuring smile. She didn't know whether he had told the truth or not. Had he accidently brushed against her shoulders or did he do it in his sleep and not realize it and was too embarrassed to admit it? Well, either way, no harm done. She wouldn't bring it up again. It would only make him feel bad if she did. And besides, even if he'd put his arm around her on purpose, it kind of felt comforting, knowing he might care enough for her to do that.

Her answer took him off the hook for now. He felt so relieved and smiled back at her. As soon as they began walking down the steps from the aircraft to the ground, they were met with heat and high humidity. Ross quickly removed the jacket he'd worn on the plane and Maribel took off her sweater. They wouldn't need those until the return flight.

They checked into the base lodging facility and after a short break, called for a taxi. As their taxi drove from Mactan Island westward towards Cebu City, crossing the Mandaue-Mactan Bridge, Ross asked Maribel the first of several questions that were on his mind.

"Is the cemetery where your mother is buried very far from here?"

"It's about a thirty minute drive, depending on the traffic. It's on Cuenco Avenue, across the river from the uptown part of Cebu City. We have to pass through the older downtown area first in order to get there. You'll see a lot of historic places in the downtown area," she informed him.

"Like what, for example?"

"Well, there's Fort San Pedro and not far from that is Magellan's Cross. Would you like to see those places after we go to the cemetery?" She'd been to both places before with her parents and wouldn't mind seeing them again, acting as a tour guide for Ross.

"Sure. I've never been here before. So, if you don't mind me asking, how long did you and your parents live here?"

"My father was stationed at Mactan Air Base on an eighteen month unaccompanied short tour. Then after he and my mother got married, his tour was extended, several times actually. We stayed here until I was six years old. We lived in an apartment building near downtown Cebu City all that time. My mother was born and raised here. She taught me how to speak her native language which is called Cebuano. I also learned to speak Tagalog and of course, English."

"Say something in Cebuano and then the same thing in Tagalog. I've never heard you speak in either of those two dialects," Ross said, just before she changed the subject.

"Unsang orasa na? That means 'What time is it?' in Cebuano. Ano oras na? That means 'What time is it?' in Tagalog. OK, enough about me now. We need to talk some more about you and use some of our time on this trip as counseling time," she reminded him.

"More psychoanalysis, you mean."

"Yes, that's right. I get the feeling you don't like talking about your childhood years and your feelings towards your parents. I'm not here to judge you, you know," she reminded him for about the tenth time it seemed.

Maribel had the taxi driver pull over once on their way to the cemetery so she could buy some freshly-cut flowers to put on her mother's grave. "Stay in the taxi, Tom. I'll be right back."

"Why do you want me to wait for you in the taxi while you get the flowers?" Ross asked inquisitively. He still had much to learn about the Philippines.

Maribel stood outside of the taxi but had not shut the rear door yet and leaned in to answer him. "I can speak to the salesperson in their language and try to barter with them for a lower price. If they see you, they might think you're my husband or boyfriend. They think all Americans have lots of money and they'll raise the price. There are two prices on just about everything when you go shopping in this country, the local's price and the American or tourist price. That's why." With that said, she shut the door and left to go buy some flowers at the local's price.

After their somber visit to the grave of Maribel's mother, another session of psychoanalysis began. It didn't bother Ross at all that the taxi driver could hear every word. Besides, they'd never see the man again and vice versa. He didn't believe that any of his childhood memories or feelings about his parents would hurt his chances of having Doctor Edwards sign off on his paperwork as being OK again, so he answered all of Maribel's questions truthfully. He knew he was normal and was deserving of a clean bill of mental health. His entire life had been very normal, until Vietnam.

Remy Minaguet left his tire repair shop on foot. It was a bright sunny day with the usual high humidity. Cebu City is only ten degrees north of the equator, with tropical weather all year long. He worked up a sweat as he quickly walked northwest to South Osmeña Boulevard, then turned left and stayed on the sidewalk of the busy street that was now full of late afternoon, early evening rush hour traffic. The exhaust fumes from hundreds of jeepneys, buses, taxis and motorcycles caused him to cover his nose with a bandana he always carried with him. Between his stomach and the waistband of his pants was a black plastic bag with enough marijuana in it to last most smokers a couple of weeks. An oversized T-shirt helped hide the bulge it created.

As Remy crossed over Legaspi Street, he could see the remains of an old Spanish fort that was built in 1565, under the command of Miguel Lopez de Legazpi. Fort San Pedro was his destination, where he hoped to meet with a young American GI and strike a deal that would net him a handsome profit.

Remy looked to his left and saw the man he was to meet with. A local taxi pulled up to the curb near the guy and a man and a woman got out and walked towards the fort. It was common for tourists on sightseeing trips to be approached by local vendors, trying to sell them postcards or trinkets of one type or another and so this drug transaction he was about to be involved in would look just like a tourist paying a vendor for a souvenir. The more people in the area, the better, as far as Remy the drug dealer was concerned.

Ross and Maribel were still on the sidewalk just outside of the entrance of Fort San Pedro because Ross wanted to read the sign that told about the history of the place. It reminded him of the metal signs with raised letters he'd seen at some historical places back in the States. Ross was standing closer to the sign than Maribel was and out of the corner of his eye to his left, he saw some movement and heard a commotion.

The young American GI, who had not given Remy his name, only what color of shirt he'd be wearing when they met, pulled out his wallet and began counting out the pesos that Remy demanded for the marijuana. Remy took the bag of weed out of his pants and held it tightly in one hand while holding out his other hand for the money.

Seemingly out of nowhere, a man with a

large old .38 caliber revolver appeared on the road-side of the two men making the drug deal. His loud voice, demanding both the cash and the drugs is what Ross heard, above the background noise of heavy traffic. From his angle, Ross thought it was an armed robbery, having no idea about the drug deal going on between an American and a Philippino. He saw one Philippino, dressed in blue jeans and a white T-shirt, holding a large pistol, and a young American he figured to be a GI because of his haircut, wearing tan shorts and a yellow T-shirt, hand him some money. The other Philippino man, wearing cut-off blue jeans and a light blue shirt that looked two sizes too big and was holding a black plastic bag tightly in one hand, suddenly dropped to the ground. He quickly opened the bag and pulled out a pistol that looked much smaller than the large .38 revolver held by the gunman trying to rob him.

As Remy nervously shot at the robber, the "pop, pop" sound of his .22 caliber pistol caused Ross to react instinctively. He sensed Maribel's position about a foot behind him and to his right and he turned, grabbed her, then pulled her to the ground with him, all in one quick motion. He made sure that he'd placed his body between her and the shooter, telling her, "Stay down! There's nowhere else to go!" Once again, his right arm was across her shoulders.

Looking around at ground level, Maribel saw that he was right. They were laying on the ground, out in the open, with no cover whatsoever and the gunfire had come from only a few feet away. It became clear to her now what was happening nearby. Her heart was beating fast and she was scared to death.

The first shot from Remy's poorly-aimed pistol had missed the robber completely and the second one barely grazed the man's arm but was enough of a shock to cause him to drop the peso bills that were now being scattered all over the ground by a light breeze. Before Remy could get off a third shot, the robber, who had led a life of crime for most of his adult life, pumped five big .38 caliber slugs into his chest. He died quickly as his lifeblood began to stain the sidewalk on both sides of his still form.

The young American took off running as soon as Remy fired the first shot. He sprinted away as fast as he could and about half a city block later, got on a jeepney that had stopped to pick up some more people who were headed home from work. He didn't care where it was headed as long as it took him far away from the gunfire. The hell with the money, he just wanted to make it back to Mactan Air Base without getting killed. He'd just have to find someone else who would sell him some "grass," as he called it.

Meanwhile, the robber quickly busied himself with picking up the pesos that lay scattered around his feet. He put the pistol behind his back, tucked under his belt. Ross saw this and the opportunity to do something. He hated to see bad guys getting away with things and no police had shown up yet. He acted again on training and instincts. Telling Maribel quietly, "Stay here," he jumped to his feet and rushed to the side of the man who lay bleeding on the sidewalk. He picked up the small pistol that was still held, now very loosely, in the dead man's hand.

That's when the robber noticed him and stopped picking up the paper bills that were still on the ground. He stood up from his bent-over position and reached for his gun, knowing there was still one bullet left. He didn't fear the other man's gun because it didn't have the stopping power of his larger caliber weapon. He could take a couple of bullets and still come out ahead and he was willing to gamble his life on it.

Ross had taken the major's advice and spent some time at the firing range to hone his marksmanship skills. He knew the .22 pistol he now held might take more than one shot to bring down a grown man, unless...

"Pop" was the last sound the robber ever heard. The single bullet fired by Ross hit him in his left eye, passed through the exploding orb, through the front and rear cerebral hemispheres and then flattened out against the interior of the skull, after cracking it. From a mere six feet away, the small target had been fairly easy to hit. The small semi-automatic pistol held more bullets in the clip but Ross had only needed one. As soon as the robber's dead body hit the hard sidewalk, the pesos once again began scattering around on the ground.

There were still no police on the scene yet and nobody except Maribel was anywhere near Ross. She was still laying on the ground about ten feet away. The noisy traffic was continuously flowing, passing by in both directions on South Osmeña Boulevard as if nothing had happened at all. Taking all of this into consideration, Ross placed the small black .22 caliber pistol back where he'd found it, in the hand of the man who'd died on the sidewalk from multiple gunshot wounds to the chest. Then he helped Maribel stand back up and suggested they leave the area quickly. The last thing he wanted was to be placed on IH, International Hold, for a long period of time while the Philippine court system decided whether or not this good Samaritan shot another man to death in self-defense. While on IH, he wouldn't be allowed to leave the country even if his tour of duty here was over.

That was the closest thing to an old Wild West shootout that Ross had ever been involved in or witnessed, unless he counted the trips he'd made as a kid from his home in Del City to an amusement park called Frontier City, a few miles away in Oklahoma City. There, he witnessed several shootouts between the good guys and bad, all adorned in Western outfits from the late 1800s, complete with realistic guns that shot blanks and filled the air with lots of smoke and noise. He saw lots of cowboys falling from buildings, horses and even trains. The stuntmen made the gunfights look so real to everyone, not just to a young, wide-eyed kid named Tom Ross.

What had occurred here today in Cebu City, Philippines would have been called "frontier justice" back in his home state a hundred years ago. His heart was still racing from the adrenaline rush his system had just experienced.

"Are you sure this is the right thing to do?" Maribel asked, as they drove away from the bloody scene in a taxi. They were picking small bits of grass from their clothes from having both been on the ground.

"I think it is, given the circumstances. I witnessed a guy robbing a man, two men actually. One of the men tried to defend himself and got shot to death by the robber, while the guy who handed over his cash, ran off. Then, when I picked up the dead man's gun and started to raise it towards the robber, with the intent of only holding him here until the police showed up, he pulled his gun out and was going to shoot me. He gave me no choice but to shoot him in self-defense. If he'd gotten off the first shot, I'd be back there now, laying dead on the sidewalk, just like the other man. And who knows? He then might have decided to kill you too," he said. "The dead man I got the gun from had already shot the robber once in the arm, so I just returned the gun to him and now he can get the credit for killing the bad guy. The man who had his money stolen ran away, so he didn't witness all the shots being fired. Did you see everything?"

"No," Maribel replied, "I didn't see it all either."

"And I doubt if any passersby in any of those vehicles driving past us saw everything either, so no witnesses. The way I see it, two innocent men were being robbed, one lost his money and the other one lost his life. The bad guy is dead now so he won't be robbing or shooting any more people to death. I'd say the end result of all this is that justice was done and I did what I had to do to stay alive myself."

Ross had his own way of explaining and simplifying things and he sounded very convincing. He still had no idea what was in the black plastic bag, other than the small black pistol the man with all the holes in his chest had produced. He was also unaware that the robber was interrupting a drug deal being conducted by two "innocent" men. Slowly, ever so slowly, his heart rate returned to normal. He hoped Maribel would see things his way and not insist on going back and explaining everything to the police.

Maribel sat next to Ross in the back seat of the taxi and tried to replay everything she'd seen and heard, in her mind. She was still a little unsettled about the whole incident, confused by her values of right and wrong in regards to waiting at the scene for the police to show up, and the explanation Ross had just given her for his actions.

In any case, it was only a short ride by taxi from Fort San Pedro to the historic site of Magellan's Cross, their next stop. Ross decided he'd just have to see the inside of Fort San Pedro some other time. Their taxi stopped across the street from Cebu City Hall, near the intersection of Santo Niño Street and D. Jakosalem Street, a short distance north of busy Quezon Boulevard. The traffic in this part of the downtown area was getting heavier by the minute it seemed, as more and more people began closing their shops and stores and headed home after a long day at work. In a few minutes, the building that housed Magellan's cross would be closed to tourists.

Ross had a déjà vu moment once again when Maribel, acting as his tour guide, now began telling him about Magellan's cross as they entered the building that housed it. He'd gone on a tour of Saigon when Genevieve was his tour guide then. Another uncanny coincidence or fate intervening?

They walked into a stone rotunda and the first thing that got his attention was the painting up on the ceiling. He stood there, looking up in utter amazement as Maribel explained what he was looking at.

"The guy over there," she began as she pointed at the painting of a Spaniard, "is Ferdinand Magellan. He looks the part of a leader in his armor with that sword, doesn't he?"

"Yes, he certainly does," Ross agreed.

"He led an expedition from Spain to the Philippines and in 1521 he had a cross erected as a sign of his Christian faith. He claimed these islands for his country and as this painting shows, it was some of the natives of these islands who actually planted the cross."

Maribel then led Ross over to a crucifix

that had been on display in the stone rotunda since 1841. "This wooden cross is said to contain pieces of the original one depicted in the painting we just saw." They both stared at it in silence for a moment, recognizing the historical significance of it.

"Whatever happened to the original one and Magellan?" Ross asked, appreciating the opportunity to see something so old and venerated. Even though he'd just witnessed a man being shot to death and had killed a man himself less than twenty minutes ago, he showed no signs of stress at all now from those violent and bloody events. He was totally focused on the relics here and the story that went with them. He was enjoying the tour that Maribel was giving him and he was living in the moment.

"I'm not sure exactly what happened to the original cross that was erected in 1521 but I do know that Ferdinand Magellan was killed a short while later that same year."

"How did he die, do you know?" an inquisitive Ross asked.

"Well, if you can wait until tomorrow, not only can I tell you, but I can also take you to the place where he was mortally wounded in a battle."

Just then, before Ross could respond, the person responsible for locking up the building, interrupted them. "I am sorry, but we have to close now," the middle-aged woman said, in fairly good English. "We will open again on Monday at 9 a.m. if you would like to come back."

"Thank you," Maribel replied. Turning to Ross, she said, "Let's get back to the base before it gets dark, Tom."

"OK, let's go. Lead the way!" he replied enthusiastically.

On the ride back to Mactan Air Base and the base lodging facility, they talked about the day's events in hushed tones so their driver couldn't hear. By the time the car stopped in front of the lodging office sign, Ross and Maribel were in agreement about his actions and tomorrow's itinerary. She had not seen enough of the robbery and shootings to be a witness against him if they ended up having to go to court and she felt good about that. Also, she was looking forward to showing Ross more of the area she and her parents used to live in.

The thing that kept her awake for a while that night as she lay all alone in bed, was the memory of that moment when Ross pulled her to the ground, when she first heard the gunfire. Things had happened so quickly that only now, as she replayed everything in slow motion in her mind, did she realize the full extent and meaning behind what Ross had done. He had pulled her to the ground to keep her from accidentally being shot and possibly killed. Then he protected her by placing his body between the shooter and herself and she felt, for the second time in twenty-four hours, that he'd put an arm around her shoulders.

Was that done out of pure instinct or were his actions guided by feelings for her, to protect her because he still felt that he'd failed to protect Genevieve? Trying to understand Ross from the point of view of a psychiatrist was one thing, but confusing her now was the reaction to his deeds from a different part of her. She'd intended to avoid developing any feelings for her patient beyond empathy but what she felt now was... confused.

What had happened today was an incident, a dangerous, even deadly one, in which she witnessed her patient acting in ways that she could only describe as being heroic in nature, not only saving her from possible harm but possibly others as well. And then he was "as cool as a cucumber," showing no signs of stress or anxiety afterwards. The last thought that went through her mind before she finally fell asleep was, "What kind of man is this?"

## CHAPTER 9

Ross and Maribel checked in at the Space-A counter of the passenger terminal at Mactan Air Base right after breakfast. Their return flight to Clark Air Base would be leaving at 2 p.m. That gave them plenty of time to visit one of Maribel's favorite places, first seen by her as a child almost twenty years ago.

"Yesterday you asked me how the famous Spanish explorer, Ferdinand Magellan, died. Do you remember that?"

Ross had not forgotten. "Yeah, I remember. And I also remember you saying that you would take me to the place where he was mortally wounded too. Is that where we're going now?"

"Yes, we're going to one of the oldest historic sites in the whole country, the

Mactan Shrine," she stated confidently. Maribel was very knowledgeable about the local history.

After a short ride by taxi off base, they were soon standing in a short line of people that were about to get in the back of a tourist jeepney that would take them there. Maribel paid the driver for two fares and two other couples, all Philippinos, joined them in the back bench seats for the ride. Many jeepneys took people on tours seven days a week because they made the most money on weekends.

Ross wished that he'd brought along an umbrella because the clouds were building up in the distance and it looked like it might rain before long. The sun was already playing peek-a-boo, hiding behind puffy white clouds overhead. The larger clouds in the distance looked dark and menacing. The light breeze did very little to ease the heavy humidity he felt already, even though it was still early in the day. Rainy season had begun throughout the islands and the chance of rain was now in each daily weather forecast. He looked at Maribel and the others and they didn't seem bothered by the high humidity at all. It was, for him, just like the weather he'd experienced this time of year in Vietnam. He just couldn't seem to adapt to it and started sweating.

On the way to their destination, Maribel began telling Ross about the historic site. She enjoyed playing the role of tour guide and she was also very happy at being back in familiar territory.

"As I mentioned before, Ferdinand Magellan was the Spanish explorer who claimed the Philippines for his king and country. He met with several chiefs of the different islands in the region and made friends with most of them by giving them gifts he'd brought from

Spain. There was one chief named LapuLapu that suspected the Spanish had come here to conquer them, not just to visit and be friends. So, on April 27, 1521, Magellan and sixty of his soldiers sailed to this island to try and persuade LapuLapu and his people to accept the Spanish."

Just then the jeepney driver announced their arrival at the Mactan Shrine and everyone got out of the colorful vehicle. It was painted in swirls of red, blue and yellow from fender to fender, with the name of the tour company in hand-painted block letters in white, against a blue background on both sides.

Maribel told Ross to wait for her while she spoke in private with the driver. She slipped the driver a few pesos after telling him that she and her friend would walk around on their own and that she would tell her friend about this place since she had gone on the tour before. The driver nodded his approval and smiled. A few extra pesos were a welcome addition to his low wages, so he didn't mind at all.

Pulling Ross by the arm, Maribel led him away from the others, much to his surprise.

"What's going on? I thought we were going on a tour." He looked at her, still not realizing what had just happened.

"We are on a tour and I'm your tour guide. Hi! My name is Maribel Edwards and today I'm going to tell you a fascinating story while I guide you around our country's oldest historic site," and having said all that in a voice that sounded like a real tour guide, she began laughing and smiling at Ross in a way that both amused him and surprised him as well.

He began with his favorite exclamation, "Well I'll be doggone," and broke into a short-lived laugh and smiled, his biggest smile in a very long time. "So you do have a sense of humor after all! Imagine that, I've got a psychiatrist and tour guide all rolled into one. This must be my lucky day for sure!" he quipped, going along with her sudden outburst of humor.

"I think this place makes me feel good because my parents brought me here and it brings back such happy memories of the three of us together," she explained. "Well, let's get started so we can finish up when the others do," she said in a light-hearted tone.

"I'm ready when you are," Ross replied. Seeing her so happy and smiling pulled at his heartstrings in more ways than one. Once again, she reminded him of Genevieve and himself when they enjoyed being together in Saigon and Cholon, and he wondered when and if these comparisons he kept making between the two women would ever stop.

"So, as I was saying, Magellan and sixty of his soldiers came here and LapuLapu and his men thought they were invaders and decided to defend their island. The natives only had knives, spears, bows and arrows as weapons but they were fierce fighters. They managed to drive the Spanish off the island, fatally wounding Magellan with a spear to his head and a poisoned arrow in one of his legs." She paused and pointed at the bottom of the stone foundation of the shrine. "Do you see that?"

"Yeah, the date: 27 April 1521," Ross replied. "Wow! That was a long, long time ago!"

"And look over there," Maribel said as she pointed towards a statue of a man. "That's supposed to be LapuLapu but I honestly don't believe that he really had such big muscles or 6-pack abs," she said with a laugh.

"I don't know about that," Ross replied, "he could have belonged to a local gym, you know!" trying to interject a little humor of his own.

"And did you know that you can find Lapu-Lapu on some of the local restaurant menus?" Maribel asked.

"What? I don't understand that at all. Did they name a sandwich after him or something?"

"Not exactly. Lapu-Lapu is also the name of a variety of fish found in the local waters."

Then they both laughed and walked slowly back to the jeepney where they joined the others, just as a few large raindrops began to fall on the metal roof over their heads and thunder sounded off in the distance.

The Lady of the Seas had left North Harbor in Manila after her owner finished his important business there. Mang Binh Hao had lightened his load of cargo quite a bit. As they drew closer to Hong Kong, he was thinking of leaving there with even less illegal cargo on board. Business was thriving these days. The Paracel Islands were to their southwest and Hong Kong was still about 350 nautical miles due north when Hao experienced some unforseen circumstances.

The South China Sea was now full of twenty foot swells and wind-driven rain was lashing at the cargo ship as a strong typhoon cut through the Luzon Strait between the Philippines and Okinawa and began curving northeastward towards the mountainous island of Taiwan. The motion of the water in Hao's king size heated water bed made love-making an enjoyable adventure, especially when his partner was a beautiful young teenager from

Hong Kong. She just happened to be hooked on heroin and was a bona fide nymphomaniac, on top of everything else, including Hao, pun intended. What caused her earlier-than-planned-for demise was her inability to not get seasick in bed.

As the naked 19-year old rode Hao's stiff stallion like a cowgirl at a rodeo bull-riding contest, she suddenly turned pale and vomited her last meal all over him, coating his torso, arms, neck and face in warm, stinking, chunks of puke. It would have been terrible enough had she just up-chucked only once but the poor girl lost all control of herself and barfed all over Hao a second time before he literally threw her off of him. Now covered in the putrid contents of what had only moments before been in the stomach of his young lover, Hao went into a rage.

He began by calling her every evil word that came to his very upset mind, cursing a blue streak in Chinese so she would understand everything. Then he threw a roundhouse right that collided with great impact against her left temple as she knelt on the bed beside him, knocking her out cold. As she lay still on his soiled sheets, with her long, dark brown hair covering most of the upper half of her naked body, Hao headed quickly to his large shower stall.

After a long, hot, steamy shower in which Hao scrubbed himself pink trying to get clean, he toweled himself off and then got dressed in some dark colored clothing that he intended on getting rid of later, after disposing of his young concubine first.

Hao used the sheets from the water bed to wrap her body in, rolling her over and over, making sure her thin arms and shapely legs were tightly wrapped. She almost looked like an Egyptian mummy by the time he was done. He doubted that she would ever breathe again as her face was now covered by several layers of sheets. Images of her pretty face ran through his mind as he bound her up tight in both the top sheet and then the fitted sheet as well. Both sheets stunk real bad from her vomit and had to be gotten rid of too.

He struggled to lift the girl's limp, sheet-wrapped body from the surface of the water bed's vinyl mattress. She wasn't really heavy, even wrapped in two sheets, but Hao wasn't very strong, especially in his condition. He'd smoked some black tar opium earlier that evening and was still under the influence of it, though to a lesser degree now than he'd been a couple of hours ago.

By the time Hao reached the ship's railing at the outer edge of the deck, he was sweating and dead-tired. It was a pitch-black night out with a strong wind blowing and heavy seas, making even this large cargo ship heave to-and-fro, up and down. With a quick look down both directions of the railing to make sure nobody was able to see him, Hao grunted and heaved the girl's body over the side. The sounds of the heavy seas against the sides of the ship and high winds combined to cover up the small splashing sound the dead weight of her body made when it hit the dark stormy waters of the South China Sea.

The hard blow to the side of her head, delivered with a strong force backed by rage, had killed her. She'd already stopped breathing even before Hao began wrapping her in the sheets. The short life of 19-year old Mai Le Chang, sold into prostitution by her parents at age 12, ended as so many of Hao's concubines had, in sudden death and a watery grave.

## CHAPTER 10

Bhoy Santos had some time on his hands, an unusual situation for this man who liked to keep himself busy. He wasn't into killing time, or wasting it, as some would prefer to say. But, he was into killing people that he thought needed killing.

Edwin Sanchez had held down the hand of AFOSI agent Travis Davis as Rico Salazar cut some of Davis' fingers off during the questioning session they held prior to killing him. It was Sanchez who had emptied two clips of M-16 rifle ammo into the 55-gallon drum that held agent Davis when they were in the Lingayen Gulf near Hundred Islands National Park. And, it was also Edwin Sanchez who had boasted to a bar girl in a sleazy strip-joint on MacArthur Highway in Angeles City one night that it was he who had shot up the metal container with an American GI in it. Too many cold beers one night while bar-hopping and the overweight former logger with a big gut and an even bigger mouth, just couldn't keep a secret.

The following night, unknown to Sanchez, a friend of Bhoy Santos, who just happened to be the bar owner of the place where he'd done his boasting, heard the story from one of his girls about the killing of the American. The next day, the bar owner paid a visit to Santos at his home.

"Ah, my friend, good to see you again," Santos greeted his long-time friend.

Rogelio San Luna had traveled in his regular size family jeep to visit Santos in his home on San Vincente Street in the suburb of Binondo, Metro Manila. They'd been classmates in school many years ago and still managed to stay in touch, even though their lives had taken very different paths.

"Good to see you too," Rogelio replied. He went by the nickname of Roger, given to him by Bhoy Santos when they were both much younger.

"So, what brings you to the big city, Roger?" Santos asked as they headed towards the main living area of the large, old house.

Roger reached for Bhoy's arm just before entering the living room and spoke in a hushed voice, "Is there somewhere we can go, just the two of us, and speak in private?"

The look of grave concern on his friend's face surprised him, causing him to stop in his tracks. He looked into Roger's eyes and somehow knew it was something serious that needed to be addressed, not the kind of thing you'd discuss around family or hired help like the yard boy or house girl that many Philippinos with a good income employed.

"Sure, let's take a ride across the river south of here," he replied, referring to the nearby Pasig River. Binondo was on the north side of it, Manila proper to the south. Santos called out to his six "handy men" from the back door. They were all sitting around in the shade of a couple of large trees in the back yard. He told them he'd be back in about an hour. He didn't say it to his men but he didn't want anyone else to hear the news his old friend was about to share with him.

Santos sat in the front passenger seat while San Luna drove. "Turn here onto Paredes Street," he told his friend, "then after we cross over Jones Bridge, go straight for a while."

Shortly after crossing over the Pasig River on Jones Bridge, they could see the outer walls of old Fort Santiago to their right and slightly ahead. Inside of the walls of the 154-acre fort was the city of Intramuros, founded in 1571 by the Spanish explorer, Miguel Lopez de Legazpi. As they traveled south on Burgos Street, they could see more of the fort on their right. There were dozens of people walking along the paths and sidewalks just outside of the thick stone walls of what was the main tourist attraction of Manila.

"Turn left here," Santos directed, "then stop when you see a small lake with water fountains in it."

They would end up on Orosa Street near Rizal Park, named after Doctor Jose Rizal. The Spanish authorities imprisoned Rizal in Fort Santiago in 1896, charging him with inciting revolution against the Spanish government. They executed him at a spot in the northwest section of the park, a short distance north of the Rizal Monument and he became the Philippine's national hero. Both Santos and San Luna had learned all about this part of Philippine history in school together and had visited this part of Manila on a school outing many years ago. Now they returned here again, still friends and on familiar grounds.

The lake and fountains Santos had referred to was listed as the Central Lagoon and Fountains on the tourist maps sold by vendors in the area. It was located due east of the Rizal Monument, which was visible from here. As both men got out of the jeep, a group of people that had gathered earlier that morning to practice t'ai chi on the soft grass of the park nearby, began breaking up and saying goodbye to eachother. It was a partly cloudy, breezy day, but not too hot and humid yet. That had made it easier for the exercise group to stay a little longer than usual.

"Let's take a walk over by the water," Santos suggested, not wanting to walk very far and not wanting to delay hearing what his friend had to say either. San Luna nodded and walked along with his friend and they soon passed a small group of men practicing a Philippino-style of stick fighting, a form of martial arts that had been around for hundreds of years, even before the Spanish took over. It was called "arnis de mano." Lots of people came to Rizal Park every day for different reasons.

"So, what is it my friend, something so secret you could not tell me in my own house?" The two men were now sitting in a grassy area near the lagoon with the water fountains.

"One of my dancers told me that a man named Edwin Sanchez, a man who said that he is a friend of yours, bragged to her about killing an American."

The news stunned Santos. "What exactly did he tell her? Anything specific, any details?" He was worried and it showed, as he looked his friend in the eyes.

"Only that he was the one who shot up a metal container that had an American GI inside of it. He had a lot of beers that night and I guess that might have made him boastful," San Luna concluded.

"What did you tell your dancer after she told you about Sanchez?" Santos inquired.

"I told her not to repeat the story to anyone and to just forget about it. You know how some people get sometimes when they have had too much to drink. They tell all kinds of stories and you can't believe most of them anyway. I'm sure she didn't tell anyone else and I'm also sure that if any of my other girls had heard the same thing they would have told me too," he reassured Santos.

He knew what businesses his friend Santos was involved in and his own bar business was under the protection of his friend as well, free of charge because of their long-standing friendship. If anyone tried to make San Luna pay for "protection," all he had to do was tell Santos and his men would make sure they never tried that again.

"Thank you, my friend. I will take care of that big mouth, Sanchez. He won't be bragging about anything to your dancers again. And by the way, is it true you get free lap dances from your girls since you own the place, Roger?" he jokingly asked, with a wink of an eye.

"Oh yes, every night if I want. Come and visit some time and I'll arrange one for you too, on the house!" San Luna replied with a big grin. And he wasn't joking either. He was dead serious. Also forty-five years old but married to one of his much-younger female employees, San Luna had enjoyed many free lap dances at his night club over the past few years, along with other "freebees."

They drove back to the Santos residence in Binondo and after dropping off his friend, Rogelio San Luna returned to Angeles City. Bhoy Santos would be passing through there in the very near future on his way to a quiet location just up the road a ways. Like Mang Binh Hao, whenever he decided to tie up loose ends, somebody died.

Just a few short miles north of Angeles City and Clark Air Base is a long winding river. There is a distinct promontory projecting high above the surrounding countryside just across the north side of the river and a short distance to the west of MacArthur Highway. The small town nearby is called Bamban and some of its residents sell food, drinks and trinkets at the foot of the hill that is topped with three wooden crosses that are visible from the highway. There is a gravel parking lot at the base of the steep hill and cement steps with metal handrails on both sides that lead up to a religious shrine that consists of a statue of the Virgin Mary and the baby Jesus in it. It's just a short walk from there to Bamban.
Adventurous hikers can leave the level ground at the shrine and step onto a narrow steep path on the right, then climb up to the very top of the hill and stand next to the three wooden crosses. The view from that spot is absolutely breathtaking. Looking southwestward, one can see the curving river nearby and the mountains looming in the distance, further to the west. To the southeast, all of Mount Arayat, the entire 1,026 meters of it, can be clearly seen.
To the left of the majestic extinct volcano, one can often see the smoke generated from the fires set to burn off the remains

of the cuttings after sugarcane has been harvested. Otherwise, the countryside all around the mountain is very flat and from the top of this steep cross-topped hill in Bamban, you can see many miles off in the distance. It's only while looking north that visibility is limited due to hills between Bamban and Capas, the next town north of there.

Below the summit of this high peak is a tunnel that goes through the entire hill, front to back. Due to a curve in the tunnel about halfway through its length, from the entranceway, one can't see the light entering the other end from the sun on a bright, cloudless day. Some locals say their grandparents used this tunnel they dug to live in and hide from the Japanese during World War II. To reach the entrance, you have to climb over the handrail to the left of the religious shrine and follow a narrow and very steep path going up about twenty-five feet higher.

Bhoy Santos and his gang arrived at Bamban around noon only two days after he learned about what Edwin Sanchez had done. One of his men stayed with the jeepney in the gravel-covered parking area at the foot of the steep hill as the rest of them walked away. Vehicle thefts were common as jeepneys were very easy to steal and so leaving one man behind was common practice.

"So, this is the place you were telling us about, Mr. Santos?" Edwin Sanchez innocently asked, unaware of the real reason for this trip.

"This is it, boys," Santos replied, as much to Sanchez as to the other four men with him. Besides himself and Sanchez, Santos had brought along Rico Salazar, Carlos Reyes, Rudy Managuet and Manny Gibanem. All of these men had been hired to do whatever "dirty work" needed to be done in the drug and protection racket businesses. Leo Cruz was keeping an eye on the jeepney.

"Let's get something to drink before we start climbing," Santos announced, as he began walking over to a small roadside stand. It was around 85° in the shade they were now standing in, under a large old tree that the vendor found as a slightly cooler and convenient location to do business in. The ten year old boy was selling cold soft drinks that were served in small plastic bags with a straw sticking out of the top, held in place by a rubber band that kept the bag pinched together around the straw. Young children in rural areas such as this often helped out in their family businesses instead of attending school. It was a fairly common practice.

Santos looked around to see if anyone else was in the area. A couple of elderly women, with small black umbrellas held over them to keep the hot sun off of their heads were half-way down the steps that led up to the religious shrine and grotto. They would be gone soon.

As soon as he saw that everyone had finished their refreshments, he spoke up. "Let's go. I want to show you all this tunnel I told you about, before it starts raining." Rain showers were common almost every afternoon now in the rainy season. Large puffy white clouds already dotted the blue sky above as they began their upward trek, taking the cement steps one at a time, with almost a hundred more to go.

Santos had told his men that an old school chum of his, told him about this tunnel and he wanted to check it out since it wasn't far from Angeles City. They were headed there later on to do some business and have a meal before heading back to Manila. He fabricated the part about Japanese soldiers possibly burying some of the loot stolen from Philippinos in the area, in the tunnel. It was the only way he thought he'd be able to get them all interested in going in the tunnel with him, especially Edwin Sanchez.

They took a short break after reaching the top of the steps and gathered around the small curved grotto-like shrine to look in amazement at the beautiful four-foot-tall statue of the Virgin Mary holding baby Jesus in her arms. Someone had hand-painted all the details of their clothing and life-like faces. Mary was dressed in a blue robe, Jesus in white. Several candles had been lit around the foot of the statue recently but a strong breeze had blown them out. Lots of melted candle wax littered the immediate area. No one said a word. It was so peaceful and very quiet up here on the hill.

Bhoy Santos thought about the irony of the situation as he noticed his men making the sign of the cross and praying. Most people came here to pray for a deceased loved one, to find solace and inner peace. He was here now, not to pray for one who was deceased, but rather, to cause one to become deceased. Very ironic indeed.

"Let's go, it's getting hot," Santos proclaimed, as he led four other men to the dark tunnel that was up the steep hillside above them. He wiped some sweat from his forehead with the back of his hand, pausing to let the slower members of the group catch up as he made his way up the steep slope.

He finally reached the entrance of the dark tunnel and peered inside. It was barely large enough to stand up in and was about six feet wide, with curved walls of dirt.

Standing in the dark entrance, Carlos

spoke up. "It looks like a cave to me. Are you sure this is the tunnel your friend told you about, Mr. Santos?" He sounded just like a skeptical child who had just learned about the Tooth Fairy.

"Of course I'm sure. Follow me." As he said that, Santos turned on a small flashlight he'd brought along and led the small group into the dark curving tunnel. The dirt floor was even and smooth and the air was a bit cooler inside. There was nothing to see but dirt, no rocks or bits of trash left behind by previous visitors anywhere. About half-way through, the tunnel curved to the left and then they could see the opening at the other end. Once outside again and in the light of day, Santos showed them the steep drop-off behind the tunnel and pointed down at the nearby river, far below. The dark tunnel was only about twenty-five yards long, so it hadn't been a very long walk.

"OK, here's the plan. Rico, you take this other flashlight with you." Santos took a small flashlight out of his pocket, identical to the small silver one he'd been using and handed it to Rico. "You, Carlos and Rudy go back to the entrance and see if you can find any place in the tunnel that looks like someone dug a hole and then covered it up again. Check the walls as well as the floor and work your way towards the middle. Use your pocket knives to dig with, if you think you found something."

Before he could finish explaining his plan, Rico asked, "What if we find something in there?"

"I'll tell you what," Santos answered, trying to keep a straight face, knowing all along they'd never find any hidden Japanese treasure or any kind of loot from World War II. "We'll split up anything you find, evenly between us, so everyone gets a share.

Fair enough?"

"That sounds good to me," Rico replied. A little bit of a lot is a lot better than nothing, he thought.

Then Santos finished telling them the rest of the plan. "Edwin and Manny will search this end of the tunnel with me and we'll all meet in the middle, OK?"

"OK," came back from the men, almost in unison.

After Rico's group left, Santos handed Manny his flashlight and told him to get started and then he'd join him in a minute after he talked to Edwin about something in private.

He then turned to Edwin as Manny walked back into the tunnel by himself. "Come over here for a minute. I've got something personal I need to talk to you about." Santos walked towards the steep drop-off a few feet beyond the back opening of the tunnel. Edwin then stood next to him, on his left, just a foot away from the edge.

Santos put his left arm around Edwin's shoulders and told him, "I want you to look me in the eye and tell me the truth, Edwin. When you were in that bar on Friday night last week, the one on MacArthur Highway in Angeles City, what exactly did you tell that girl you spent so much time with? Do you remember telling her about the American GI you killed in the metal drum out in the waters of the Lingayen Gulf?"

Edwin felt scared now. How the hell had Mr. Santos found out he'd said anything at all about that incident to anyone? He did not even remember telling that girl much of anything. Friday night was one big blur to him now as he tried to think of an answer. He looked his boss in the eye and said truthfully, " I really don't know. I don't remember much of anything about last Friday night, Mr. Santos. Honestly, I don't." He hoped Mr. Santos believed him and wouldn't be mad at him. He needed his job. It was the best paying job he'd ever had.

"You told that girl, no, you boasted to that girl all about how you shot and killed that American GI, that's what you did," Santos told him, with a bitterness in his voice. "And for that, I've got to let you go." No sooner had the last word left his lips then his left arm moved off of Edwin's shoulders.

Edwin thought that, "I've got to let you go," meant that he'd just been fired and his heart sank because he really needed the work to pay his bills. He furrowed his brows and frowned and looked away from the face of Santos, that now had a frown on it too. He looked down at the scenic, winding river far below and wondered what he'd do now that he'd been fired.

Santos put his old, heavy .38 caliber revolver up to Edwin's rib cage and pulled the trigger before the man knew what was happening. The loud **BANG** reverberated off of the back side of the hill but there was no one in that direction to hear it echo off in the distance. The bullet tore through both of Edwin's lungs and heart, killing him instantly. The impact of the projectile threw him sideways, away from Santos, and the momentum of his two hundred pound body falling sideways and down, carried him over the edge of the sharp drop-off.

As Santos watched Edwin's bloody torso bounce and roll and tumble through the brush, weeds and rocks towards the foot of the steep hill, Manny soon joined him, followed by the other men a few seconds later. By the time they arrived at the drop-off, Edwin's twisted corpse had stopped moving and was totally out of sight. No one uttered a single word as Santos returned his gun back in the waistband of his pants in the small of his back.

Santos moved away from the edge of the drop-off and told the men standing before him, "I had to get rid of Edwin before he talked any more and got us all in trouble. He told a bar girl in Angeles City what happened to the American GI he killed in the Lingayen Gulf. I've told you all before and I'll say it again, never, ever tell anyone about our business, or you'll end up dead like Edwin. Do I make myself clear?" He glared at the others and watched them all solemnly shake their heads in acknowledgement. "Let's get the hell out of here before the police show up," he instructed.

As the men turned to follow their leader back through the dark tunnel, a thin bolt of pink and white lightning flashed nearby and the CRACK of thunder that soon followed sounded just like a loud gunshot, but much louder than the actual gunshot that had preceded it a few moments before. Many more sounds of thunder would rumble throughout the area before the afternoon was over. That was why anyone who may have heard the shot that ended the life of Edwin Sanchez would have thought it was a clap of thunder. Nature had provided the perfect cover.

CHAPTER 11

Clark Air Base was located near Angeles City and it was primarily a U.S. Air Force installation. Subic Bay Naval Base and Cubi Point Naval Air Station were both located near the city of Olongapo, about 50 miles southwest of Angeles City, on the coast, next to the South China Sea. These two bases were primarily U.S. Navy installations and both had U.S. Marines assigned there as well.
It was estimated that around 135 million dollars a year was made in Angeles City and Olongapo by brothels, bars, massage parlors and other related businesses, mainly due to U.S. servicemen. Dozens of mixed-race illigitimate children were born in those two cities each year because of the liaisons between bar girls, also known as hostesses,

and American military and civilian personnel either living in or visiting the area.

As if the local military and civilian police didn't have enough problems to contend with already, an influx of military personnel on temporary duty from other American units from around the world and some of their allies, also spent time on these bases and in the nearby towns. Some of the problems caused by American GIs got the AFOSI unit at Clark Air Base involved.

"Come in and have a seat, Tom," the detachment commander said.

"What have you got for me today?" Ross asked his boss. It had been a while since he'd taken over the case of a former detachment member and a couple of other cases as well. He was looking forward to a new challenge.

Major Fred Dickinson was sitting at ease in his dark wood-paneled office. The dark color of the wood paneling made it seem much darker than it actually was. "I just wanted to let you know about the results of some of your recent investigations and to congratulate you on another job well done. Keep this up and I'll be putting you in for a Commendation Medal." He always looked forward to giving out awards at the monthly Commander's Call. He saw a small grin appear on Ross' face with the mention of the medal.

The grin was just a delayed reaction to the news Ross had been waiting for more than anything else, the results of his recent investigations. He really didn't care all that much for medals. The only one that really meant something, to him anyway, was the Congressional Medal of Honor. All the others paled in comparison and he knew he'd never do something in this line of work to earn that one.

"So, how did it go, sir?" Ross figured it must have gone well but was just being polite, looking forward to hearing all the details. Since taking over Lieutenant Davis' case, he'd been a very busy man.

Dickinson began reading from a paper in a folder on his desk. "Two 51st Tactical Fighter Wing Airmen, Franklin Potts and Thomas Smalls, both from Osan Air Base in the Republic of South Korea, were on leave in the Philippines when apprehended by AFOSI personnel assigned to Clark Air Base. They were convicted by special courts-martial for writing more than $4,550 in bad checks at various facilities on the base. Most of that money was then converted to pesos off base and used to buy drugs." He paused to see the reaction from Ross but got only questions.

"How about the two locally-assigned guys I collared? What happened to them?"

"A lot. Listen to this," the major said and then began reading again. "An Airman from the 3rd Civil Engineering Squadron, Edward Allen, was sentenced to thirty days confinement and a bad conduct discharge after pleading guilty to writing ten bad checks totalling $2,250. An Airman First Class from the 374th Aerial Port Squadron, Deon Johnson, was sentenced to reduction to Airman Basic, sixty days confinement and forfeiture of $400 per month for four months after pleading guilty to writing thirty-two bad checks totalling $2,750. And then it goes on to say," as he turned the page over to read the other side, "According to the investigating agent assigned to the local Air Force Office of Special Investigations at Clark Air Base, both men used the money from the bad checks to pay the bar fines of girls they dated off base, to pay hotel bills they accumulated in a week of partying in bars on Fields Avenue in Angeles City and to pay for the marijuana they and their dates smoked. So, that's what they told you, huh? They spent all that money on bar fines, hotels and pot?"

"That's where most of their money went. They also spent some on food, beer, transportation, movies, stuff like that. They made it sound like they were college students on spring break. I bet they regret it now though," Ross finished with a sigh, shaking his head. "Ah, misguided youth!"

A head suddenly appeared in the major's doorway just as he and Ross were wrapping things up. "Sir, excuse me for interrupting but you gotta come and see this. It's unbelievable!" the orderly room clerk told Major Dickinson. The sergeant looked really excited about something.

"What is it, Sergeant St. Claire?"

"They're showing dozens of boats full of Vietnamese landing at different places in the Philippines. There must be tens of thousands of people stuffed into all those boats. It's on TV now, sir. Check it out!"

The sergeant led the way to the break room at the end of the hall where a small portable color TV sat on top of a waist-high refrigerator. Sergeant St. Claire picked up the cup of coffee he'd left behind and took a sip. Pointing at the TV screen, he said, "See what I mean? That's Subic Bay Navy Base there and an old LST just docked with a full load of Vietnamese on it. They said that after Saigon fell to the North Vietnamese Army, these people fled the country any way they could. They said some of these Vietnamese had worked for Americans at different bases and were afraid the Communists would kill them if they found out they had worked for us." He was almost out of breath now, having talked excitedly for awhile. The caffeine he drank all day long had a lot to do with the way he talked too.

By now the small break room was crowded and Major Dickinson asked Sergeant St. Claire to turn up the volume. Sure enough, reports were coming in from different locations in the Philippines, Hong Kong, Thailand and Singapore of many boats of all types and sizes, filled to capacity and even overloaded with Vietnamese who were now being referred to as refugees.

It didn't seem all that long ago when their own President Nixon resigned from office and then eight months after that, they'd all watched the evacuation by helicopter of the U.S. Embassy in Saigon. Now they watched another historical event being played out on TV as hundreds of boats overcrowded with women, children and extended families from South Vietnam, began landing on the shores of many countries around the South China Sea, some docking only fifty miles away from them.

A few minutes later the major and Ross returned to the major's office that was long overdue for an interior decorator upgrade. Even builders of mobile homes had already stopped using the passé dark wood paneling.

"I know your investigation of Davis' old case has resulted in some GIs being apprehended," Dickinson stated. "Any breaks yet on drug dealers? You've caught some of the buyers and users but what about the dealers? It would be nice if we could get hold of some of those characters."

"As a matter of fact, I just got a new lead yesterday. It kind of fell into my lap you might say."

"Oh yeah? What can you tell me about it? I could use some more good news," Dickinson said, as he began to sip on the hot coffee he'd just gotten from the break room a few minutes ago.

Ross preferred his caffeine cold and had grabbed an orange soda from the break room's refrigerator. "I don't have my notes with me so I'll have to tell you what happened without any names. I've developed a good rapport with some security police guys who work in the Town Patrol section off base. One of them is a young single guy who has developed a friendly relationship with one of the go-go dancers at a club down on MacArthur Highway, somewhere near Fire Empire, in that part of town. He is a pretty smart kid because he never tells anyone he's a cop and he finds ways of getting information that's helpful to some of our cases." He paused to take a drink from the can of cold soda he held. He'd been talking so much that his mouth felt like it was dried out.

"Anyway, he recently told me that his girl told him a story about a drunk Philippino who bragged to her about shooting an American GI that was inside of a metal container. He gave me the guy's name and that's what I'm following up on now. The way I figure it, the guy who killed Davis must have known that Davis was on to something big in his drug investigation. So, if I can find this guy, it might lead me to a big drug dealer, in addition to Davis' killer.

Major Dickinson nodded, thought a moment, then asked, "What's your next move then?"

"I've already checked with the local police and they have nothing on this guy. They suggested I check with the National Police Headquarters in Manila." Ross looked at his boss, waiting for some kind of a reply. What he heard, however, was not what he expected.

"I've got no problem with you going to Manila but I'm curious about your psychoanalysis sessions too. How are those going these days?" Dickinson was hoping for a 100% clearance on Ross from Doctor Edwards soon. It seemed to him that these counseling sessions had been dragging on for a very long time and surely must be nearly over. Putting Ross on a dangerous case as this one was, well, it was CYA time. He had too much to lose if Ross couldn't handle the stress that this type of a job sometimes put on a person.

Ross felt sure now that Dickinson had no idea that he'd recently killed a man in Cebu City and he wasn't about to tell him either. Justice had been served as far as he was concerned. Had Dickinson known about the shooting, it would have changed everything, and not in a good way either.

"As much as I dislike having to explain everything about my childhood and my feelings and my relationship with my parents, I think it's been going well. By the time these sessions are all over, my shrink will know me better than anyone ever has, that's for sure. Thank God it's about over. Hell, my wife didn't even ask me about some of the personal things I've been asked about, but like I said, it's going well and my counseling sessions are about over." Ross had a look of pride and satisfaction about him as he returned his commander's stare. Looking his boss in the eyes emphasized the truth in his statements.

He hadn't even hesitated or given it a second thought about calling Maribel Edwards "my shrink." It simply wasn't a derogatory term to him. After all she'd done for him, he wouldn't dare be disrespectful towards her in any way. To him, "my shrink" was no different than saying, "my dentist" or "my banker," no matter how it may have sounded to others. That's just the way he was, plain and simple.

Dickinson nodded, happy that he'd soon have Ross on board, free and clear of any "baggage" from his past. "OK then, just be careful," was all Dickinson told Ross before Ross left his office.

In no time at all, a huge humanitarian effort was made to house thousands of Vietnamese refugees in some of the empty barracks at Clark Air Base that had been scheduled for renovation. When those quickly filled up, dozens of tents were erected to house the overflow. When no more refugees could be taken care of due to overcrowding, thousands of them were sent to Guam, Wake Island and other American bases in the Pacific.

Some of the young Vietnamese women that were temporarily housed in the old barracks buildings and tents were former prostitutes and drug "mules" for the dealers. A few of them hid black tar heroin inside of their body cavities as well as in their purses and luggage. It didn't take long before some of them turned to prostitution again and some GIs were lured into buying and using the lower-priced drugs the women had smuggled in. When the authorities finally caught on, body cavity searches were done and in addition to finding some heroin, diamonds, gold coins and even some gold jewelry was discovered hidden inside some of the women.

A member of Ross' AFOSI detachment was assigned to help the security police find any contraband and interview people. Ross asked his co-worker, Captain Ron Chambers, if he would ask the Vietnamese if any of them knew a man named Mang Binh Hao. He still wanted to find out if Hao had anything to do with his wife's death. Since some of the refugees had worked for American organizations in their own country, there was no shortage of interpreters.

One of the prostitutes that had been searched and questioned, told Chambers that Mang Binh Hao made it out of South Vietnam on one of his ships, along with his wife and many wealthy Vietnamese and Chinese businessmen and their families, most of them from the Cholon area. She went on to say that, because Hao had done business with the former president of South Vietnam, he knew the Communists would come after him and take away everything, maybe even his life too. So, along with many others who had worked in some way for the American government or the South Vietnamese government, he left.

Captain Chambers left a note at the office for Ross, telling him to join him at the refugee camp as soon as he could. Ross met with him the very next day.

"Hey, Ron, what have you found? Anything about this guy I'm looking for?" Ross was hoping for some good news.

Chambers invited Ross to have a seat in the large green military wall tent that served as his office. A generator supplied the power for the fan, tiny refrigerator, electric typewriter and bare lightbulb that hung from the pole in the center of this tent and all the other tents in the area they now referred to as "tent city."

"I hate to have to tell you this but, according to one young woman we interviewed, the man you were looking for, Mang Binh Hao, well, he and a bunch of wealthy business people got on a ship he owned and made it out of the country. She had no idea where they might be headed."

"Aw, crap!" was all Ross said in reply to the bad news. He was hoping that Hao might turn up here or at one of the other refugee camps in the country.

"But, I do have a surprise for you,"

Chambers said. "Wait here for a second, I'll be right back."

He got up and walked quickly towards another tent nearby. He returned with two Vietnamese women, one of them being his interpreter. Even though both females were wearing sandals, black silk pants and white cotton shirts, Ross recognized the other lady immediately and stood up with a big smile on his face.

Chambers did the first introduction. "Captain Ross, I'd like you to meet my interpreter, Miss Le. Miss Le, this is Captain Ross." The two came face-to-face and bowed, then shook hands. Ross towered over Miss Le, who was even shorter than Mai, Henri Ferrand's maid. Henri had been his wife's father, dying shortly before their wedding from a cancerous brain tumor.

"Pleased to meet you, Miss Le."

"I am pleased to meet you too, Captain Ross," she replied.

Miss Le moved over to one side and said, "I believe you two already know eachother," and before she could say another word, forgetting all about Vietnamese customary greetings, Ross bent over and gave Mai a big hug.

Mai had recognized Ross right away, mainly due to the fact that he was the only Westerner she'd ever met that wore tan cowboy boots and a wide, tan, leather belt with a large silver belt buckle, which he wore now. She still called him "American cowboy" behind his back.

Miss Le interpreted as Mai began to cry and sob out a story as soon as Ross stopped hugging her and patting her on the back, telling her how happy he was to see her again. She was constantly saying she was sorry. First, Mai told Ross that the reason she suddenly left the Ferrand house without telling anyone was because, while helping Genevieve unpack the things she had moved from their small place in Cholon to her father's house, Mai accidently discovered the Buddhist good luck charm, the colorful cloth that had been given to Ross and Genevieve in a special ceremony.

After hearing that interpreted for him, Ross had Miss Le explain to Mai that Genevieve and her uncle, her father's younger brother, had died when the Viet Cong blew up the passenger bus they had been riding in on the way back from Vung Tau after they buried her father next to her mother in the family cemetery.

That brought on even more tears from Mai. She broke down completely and cried out hysterically, explaining between sobs that it was all her fault, even though she had no knowledge of the bus explosion or the death of Genevieve and her uncle until now.

"She said it was all her fault?" Ross asked Miss Le, in disbelief. "How could it be all her fault? Was she working for the Viet Cong?" He was upset now too after hearing Mai claim that his wife's death was all her fault. How? Why? He waited for the interpreter to talk to Mai so he could find out exactly what she meant. His heart was racing in anticipation as he waited for some answers.

Miss Le spoke to him slowly, trying to get the words just right, changing a story told to her in Vietnamese into English. It had been hard for her to understand everything Mai had said because of all her crying and sobbing.

"Mai say, nobody can look at Buddhist good luck charm, only husband and wife. It made special for them. When cloth fall to floor and open, it show special message to married couple. She look at it before she put back in Genevieve's folded clothes, then realize what it was. Bad luck, very bad luck, anyone look. That why, it her fault Genevieve die, because she look at something Buddhist monk make only for husband and wife to see. It good luck only for them if nobody else see. That why Mai so upset. She say, she no VC, no VC. She very sorry."

Oh my God, Ross suddenly realized. A Vietnamese superstition about a Buddhist good luck charm for husbands and wives has caused Mai to think that she is personally responsible for the deaths of Genevieve and her Uncle Pierre.

"Miss Le," he said, almost pleading with her, "please tell Mai that she is not to blame. She did nothing wrong. The VC killed Genevieve and her uncle. It's not her fault at all. I'm not mad at her, not even a little bit. Please tell her that I'm very happy to see her again." Then he smiled at Mai, hoping to convince her.

Mai wiped her eyes dry with a small, dainty, pink handkerchief after Miss Le told her what Ross had said. Then she bowed towards him, saying, "Cam on ong, cam on ong," the Vietnamese words for "thank you, thank you."

Remembering that Mai could speak French and that Genevieve had taught him some, Ross wanted to speak directly to her without the help of an interpreter. He felt that he could tell her better in French than he could with his limited, and often mispronounced, Vietnamese. He reached out and held Mai's hand and said, "Die vous garde, mon ami. Merci beaucoup."

His words brought a smile to Mai's distraught face. She recognized instantly that he'd said, "God keep you, my friend. Thank you very much."

Ross thanked Miss Le and Captain Chambers and told them all goodbye. He had to get back to work again but was very thankful to have seen Mai once more. He was happy for her to have gotten away from Vietnam on a boat but he felt sad for her at the same time. He couldn't begin to imagine what it must have been like for her to carry around all that guilt about something that Americans knew so little about when it came to Vietnamese and Buddhist beliefs and also having to leave your own war-torn country, possibly forever, with hardly more than the clothes on your back. His visit to "tent city" was another rude awakening about life in Southeast Asia during these troubled times.

CHAPTER 12

Ross decided to call Maribel Edwards late one afternoon. He had to cancel his next appointment with her because he wasn't sure how long he was going to be in Manila, checking with the police there about a Philippine national named Edwin Sanchez.
"Hello, Maribel? Hi, this is Tom Ross."
"I know who you are, Tom, I recognized your voice. How are you today?"
"Fine. Listen, the reason I'm calling is because I have to cancel my appointment tomorrow."
"Why? Is something wrong?"
"No, everything's fine. I have to go to Manila on business and I'm not sure how long I'll be there. It could be a trip of only a few hours or it could take all day, I'm not sure. Anyway, I thought I'd better call now

to let you know."

"OK, well, that's too bad. I was planning on taking you to a nice place for your last counseling session." Her voice sounded a bit disappointed because she really was. These sessions conducted at different locations had been more fruitful than the ones done in her office and it made her job a lot easier whenever he felt less intimidated to open up about his personal life.

He asked her out of curiousity, "Where were we going if I didn't have to cancel?"

"Well, to be honest with you, I need to go to the American Embassy in Manila to get a new passport and I thought that I could do that and then show you around Manila some while we finish your last psychoanalysis session, kind of like that old saying, kill two birds with one stone."

Ross thought she still sounded somewhat disappointed. He thought it over for a second and then came up with an idea.

"What time do you have to be at the embassy? I think maybe your original plan may still work." He was hoping it would. While he really didn't like answering so many personal questions during psychoanalysis, he did enjoy sightseeing and learning about the Philippines. Plus, his tour guide was easy on the eyes, intelligent and spoke multiple languages, which came in mighty handy sometimes.

"As long as I get there before four, otherwise I'll have to spend more money on a hotel room, restaurants and more taxi fares going back there the next day. Why? What do you have in mind?" He'd sounded hopeful about her original plan so she hoped things could still be worked out too.

"I'm not on a strict schedule so let's do this. I've got the use of a government car so if you don't mind riding with me to

National Police Headquarters in Manila where I have to try and get some information about a certain Philippine national, that should not take very long. Then we can go wherever you were planning on taking me to in your original plan. After that, we head over to the U.S. Embassy so you can get your new passport and then we return to the base. How does that sound?"

"That sounds fine to me. Can you pick me up in front of the hospital at eight?"

"Sure thing. Should I bring my camera along?"

"Oh yes. Definitely bring your camera and some comfortable walking shoes. There are some places to see that will require lots of walking. See you at eight then. Bye!" She didn't think that his feet could stand a lot of walking on the sidewalks of the big city in those cowboy boots he always seemed to be wearing.

What she didn't know was, Ross could wear his boots and out-walk and even out-run most men wearing tennis shoes. He'd been wearing boots since he was three years old. There were still a few things she hadn't learned about Ross yet, even though she now had more in-depth knowledge about him than all of his family and relatives put together.

Ross was able to find out a few things about Edwin Sanchez at National Police Headquarters because they had a record of his arrests and a list of known affiliates. One of those affililiates was Bhoy Santos. The police were already investigating Santos for dealing drugs and racketeering.

It just so happened that one of the policemen working there was a cousin of Bhoy Santos. He and Ross came up with a plan, a sort of sting operation, to lure Santos into a trap so he could be apprehended. The way Ross explained his views, if Edwin Sanchez was the killer of First Lieutenant Travis Davis, and Sanchez was known to hang out with Bhoy Santos, then there was a good chance that Santos was somehow involved in the murder of the Air Force OSI agent as well. The Philippine authorities agreed with that hypothesis. A plan was soon agreed upon.

Sergeant Ricardo Santos, the cousin of Bhoy Santos, would call his cousin and tell him that another American OSI agent was looking into his business and had been to National Police Headquarters, looking into the criminal records of Edwin Sanchez. He would give his cousin a description of the American and tell him that he'd be at the U.S. Embassy around 4 p.m. that afternoon.

When that plan was acted upon, Bhoy Santos took the bait, "hook, line and sinker." He thanked his cousin, Ricardo, for tipping him off and then briefed his gang of thugs about his plans to kidnap, question, torture and eventually kill another American GI. They'd be waiting for him outside of the U.S. Embassy in Manila at 4 p.m.

"What took you so long?" Maribel asked, having waited in the visitor's lounge for over an hour as Ross conducted his business in the National Police Headquarters building.

"Sorry about that. It took them awhile to find the files on a person I needed some information about. I'm done now, so let's go." That's all she needed to know, he thought to himself. The less she knew, the better off she'd be.

They walked out of the large, old building which was a white stone and masonry structure that was repaired shortly after the end of World War II. The city of Manila had been devastated by heavy fighting that resulted in the destruction of most of the buildings and this one had been heavily damaged, requiring lots of repairs in order to be used again.

As Ross and Maribel walked to their car, the sun shone brightly in a clear, blue sky, with only a few scattered, small, puffy white clouds that were far apart. The heat and humidity still had a ways to rise yet and so the day began as a mild one for this time of year. It was the rainy season now, with afternoon rain showers and thunderstorms always a possibility. It was the start of a beautiful day for sightseeing.

Maribel was dressed appropriately for both the weather and the walking. She wore a short sleeve, white, button-up, cotton blouse, form-fitting, tailor-made blue jeans with white socks and white tennis shoes. She carried a small black leather shoulder bag on her left shoulder and wore stylish sunglasses with white plastic frames. Her long dark brown hair was combed straight, half-way down her back. Ross thought she looked very nice, especially the part of her that was made more evident in those tight, form-fitting jeans.

He, on the other hand, looked like a cowboy to all the Philippinos who gawked at him wherever he went, straight out of a Western movie featuring a cattle drive. All he needed now were a pair of spurs, a ten-gallon hat and a holstered six-shooter to complete the picture. He wore a light gray pull-over polo shirt with two buttons undone and a collar, light blue, heavily-worn blue jeans with his favorite wide, tan belt with a large silver belt buckle that had his initials engraved in it and matching tan leather Western-style boots. As was his custom, he wore no hat but did have on some silver-framed aviator sunglasses.

The first place they drove to after leaving the police headquarters was Fort

Santiago. Maribel acted as his navigator, giving him the directions he needed to travel along the east side of the centuries-old Spanish fort first, then along the south side. Ross found a place to park on Orosa Street, on the east side of Rizal Park.

"Is the traffic always this heavy?" he asked, as he reached for his camera just before exiting the car. He'd never driven in Manila before and so far it had been an adventure, to say the least.

"It gets worse at the end of the day," came the reply. "Are you ready to do some walking? There are lots of things to see in this part of the city," Maribel stated.

"Sure! You're my tour guide today. Lead the way!" he said, enthusiastically.

Ross tried his best to hide his nervousness. In a few hours, he was going to be in a precarious situation, acting as the lure to catch a well-known drug dealer and possible murderer as well. If that's what it took to bring to justice the man who may have been responsible for the death of a fellow agent, then so be it. He was willing to give it a try, even though he felt a little bit uneasy about the plan.

Instead of American police setting the trap, it was unfamiliar Philippine police and that's what made him feel nervous. He didn't know what to expect since he'd never worked with any of them before. It was the fear of the unknown that lurked in the back of his mind. Keeping the plan a secret from Maribel also made him uncomfortable on a different level, even though it was for her own good.

"This large open space we're in now is just a small part of Rizal Park," Maribel began, "named after the Philippine's national hero. The big building on our left is the National Library. To our right you can see a lagoon with water fountains. Far up ahead of us is the Rizal Monument. Back to the right of us, on the other side of the lagoon is an open-air auditorium. You see those people far off to our right, the ones sitting down and facing eachother?" She was pointing towards them for Ross to see.

"Yes, I can just barely see them," he replied.

"They're playing chess in an area known as Chess Plaza. Do you play chess?"

"No, but my grandfather taught me how to play a mean game of checkers," he joked.

She laughed a little bit at his humor. "People come to this park to do lots of different things. Some just find a shady spot under a tree to read a book or take a nap or..."

"Or make out with a loved one," Ross interjected as he pointed towards a young high school aged couple kissing and snuggling in the shade of a very large tree that he and Maribel were walking by.

"Yes, that too," she laughed as she noticed what he was pointing at.

After a few minutes of walking in a westerly direction, they came upon the tall Rizal Monument. A short distance beyond it was busy Roxas Boulevard and lots of noisy traffic.

"Let me have your camera and I'll take your picture while you stand in front of the monument. You need something to show your parents back in Oklahoma." Maribel was now more knowledgeable about his parents and his younger years growing up in Del City, Oklahoma than his wife had been due to all the time she'd spent with Ross during his grief counseling sessions and psychoanalysis.

After taking his picture with the small instamatic camera, she suggested, "Let's walk over there," as she pointed north,

"and see the site of Rizal's execution."
As they arrived by a black granite wall inscribed with Rizal's poem, <u>My Last Farewell</u>, Maribel became the tour guide again.

"Doctor Jose Rizal was executed by firing squad here at dawn on December 30, 1896. He'd been locked up in the prison inside of Fort Santiago. The Spanish held a trial which was closed to the public and found him guilty of formenting rebellion. When they held a public execution, Doctor Rizal became a martyr for the cause of Philippine independence from hundreds of years of Spanish rule." She looked at Ross then to see any impact this information may have had on him.

"Well, I can certainly understand why they built a monument and named a park after him. He was quite a man," he finally declared after a long pause of reflective silence.

"Yes, indeed he was. It's just a short walk from here to some beautiful ornamental gardens, some people call the Chinese Gardens. Would you like to go see them?"

"Sure, let's go!" he said as he fell in step with her.

After walking through the beautifully manicured, colorful gardens, they turned west towards Roxas Boulevard, then headed north across Burgos Street, stopping just long enough for Maribel to take a photo of Ross standing at the foot of the Legazpi statue. She told Ross that the statue was of the Spanish conquistador, Miguel de Legazpi.

"He led an expedition from Spain to the Philippine Islands in 1565 and from then until 1898, the islands were under control of the Spanish Crown, a total of 333 years of Spanish colonial rule." He was getting a history lesson about the Philippines today and he was enjoying it along with all the historical sights.

They left the government car where it was parked and took a short jeepney ride north on Bonifacio Drive, getting off near the Rizal Shrine, on the north side of Fort Santiago. It took them a couple of hours to see most of the sights within the thick walls of the large Spanish fort, most of Intramuros, the city within, having been mostly destroyed in World War II. About the only original building built by the Spanish that wasn't destroyed was San Agustin Church, built between 1587 and 1606. Ross was in open-mouthed awe as he viewed the intricate frescoes on the vaulted ceiling, causing him to compare it to one of Michelangelo's works of art in Italy.

A lot of the thick walls of the old fort and most of the buildings inside of it had to be rebuilt following the war. That included the building where Jose Rizal was incarcerated before the Spanish executed him.

Ross and Maribel ate a late lunch in the Ristorante delle Mitre, near the intersection of General Luna Street and Real Street in Intramuros. They had just come from San Agustin Museum nearby, where Ross had made a comment to Maribel about how he thought the ivory statue called the Immaculate Conception appeared a little Chinese-looking to him. She just smiled, nodded and didn't reply, not wanting to spoil his fun.

They ate a light meal of pancit, lumpia and stir-fried rice. The menu explained in English, for the benefit of the many English-speaking tourists from all over the world that came here, what each menu item was. For example, Ross found out that pancit was stir-fried noodles, lumpia was spring rolls, either vegetarian or with pork, shrimp, beef or chicken inside. Their ice teas were served with a slice of lime attached to the lip of the glass.

"Well, what do you think about the things you've seen so far today?" Maribel asked, playing the role of tour guide once again.

"I'm impressed! So much history, so many amazing things to see and so many people with so much traffic too. Holy cow, there must be several million people living in Manila," Ross exclaimed.

"Over eight million," she responded. "Do you like the food? I tried to order us something most people find tasty and that's not too heavy since we still have some more walking to do."

"Yeah, everything you ordered was real good. I'll have to eat out more often so I can try some of the other things on the menu sometime. What was it you said when the waitress brought the food to our table?" He hadn't learned more than a few basic words of Tagalog, the main dialect spoken here and at Clark, and was eager to learn some more.

"You mean, 'Kain na tayo?' (pronounced kaa-in na tie-o). That means, 'let's eat!' Is that what you're asking about?" she asked with a smile.

"Yes, that's it. The food here smells so good and I was really hungry too. You didn't have to tell me 'let's eat!' twice," he quipped.

Maribel could tell by his demeanor that he'd made good progress towards normality. That's what she looked for in his facial expressions, body language and everything he said. She had never studied anyone so thoroughly before and she was becoming more convinced than ever that she had done well in helping her patient through his very traumatic experience.

The only thing that concerned her now was

the way he looked at her sometimes. It was as if he was seeing someone he thought he'd seen before but wasn't quite sure. He had described his wife in great detail to her so Maribel was aware that she, like Genevieve, was half-Asian and half-Caucasian. Maybe he was mentally making comparisons or seeing something in her that reminded him of his deceased wife. Whatever the reason, she'd noticed it but wasn't upset or uncomfortable, just concerned, and decided not to mention it to him. At least not now.

By the time they got back to the car, the skies had clouded up quite a bit. They could hear a rumble of thunder off in the distance to the southeast. A large thunderstorm, producing lots of lightning, was over the hills near Antipolo and headed in their general direction. The traffic was much heavier now than it had been earlier in the day and Ross had a hard time finding a place to park near the U.S. Embassy. It was located on the west side of Roxas Boulevard, near the west end of United Nations Avenue. He ended up having to park a couple of blocks away, near Hotel Miramar, due east of their destination.

As they walked towards the gated embassy compound, Ross looked around to see if he could spot some of the Philippine National Police or anyone else who appeared to be looking at him. He didn't spot anything out of the ordinary. That was a good thing. It was now 3:45 p.m. and he wanted to get Maribel safely into the secure embassy building.

They both showed the Marine guard at the gate their ID cards and then Ross surprised Maribel. "I'll wait for you out here, OK? I think I may have left my window open in the car and if it starts raining, I'll have to run back and close it. If I'm inside the building with you, I won't be able to tell if it's raining until it's too late." He hoped she believed him.

It sounded like a plausible explanation to Maribel even though it surprised her with its suddenness. "OK. I'll meet you just outside this door then, right after I get my new passport. It shouldn't take but a few minutes."

Ross opened the door to the embassy for her and then did an about-face, heading out to the sidewalk on the other side of the iron gate. He didn't like being the target of people thought to be killers but he and the people he spoke with at the National Police Headquarters all agreed that he'd be kidnapped before being killed and the trap was now set, at least he hoped it was. He still hadn't seen anyone wearing any kind of police uniform, no Metro Manila police, no Philippine Constabulary or National Police either for that matter, as his eyes continued to look all around.

He tried his best not to look nervous, even though he was. He looked up and down busy Roxas Boulevard and watched as hundreds of vehicles of all types and sizes go past him in both directions. The exhaust fumes from all that traffic was starting to be very noticeable and so was the noise. The sidewalk was clear in both directions. That gave him some comfort. He felt a trickle of sweat go down his back as he shifted his weight from one foot to the other. It was very hot and humid and about to get even more humid because of an approaching line of thunderstorms.

As Ross looked to his left towards the north, a south-bound jeepney, as colorful and as decorated as any others he'd seen, this one with a silver horse hood ornament, pulled up to the curb and stopped right in front of him. Seeing people sitting in the side-facing bench seats in the back caused him to think that it was a regular passenger jeepney just like all the other ones he'd already seen today. And, just like a regular taxi, they would stop almost anywhere to let passengers off or pick up more.

Suddenly, the front seat passenger got out and walked directly towards him. He looked to be in his forties, about five foot four, maybe five-five, wearing blue jeans, a white T-shirt and had a red bandana tied around his head. Most noticeable was the .38 caliber revolver he held down at his side. At the same time, six more men approached Ross from the rear of the jeepney. One of them held a pillowcase and a roll of gray duct tape while the others each held a pistol of various calibers.

Reacting quickly as planned, Ross took a few steps backwards until his back was up against the iron gate of the embassy compound front entrance. He didn't dare reach for the pistol he'd hidden in his right boot. He just had to remain calm and hope the cavalry would show up soon with blaring bugles.

This was not a Chinese Kung-Fu movie where the hero is surrounded by twenty black-clad villains, where he somehow manages to defeat them all with one swift kick of the foot at a time. This was real life and in real life, if you don't do things just right, you die.

A vision of a bullet-riddled 55-gallon drum with the body of Lieutenant Davis inside popped into his mind as Ross felt himself being grabbed by several hands.

All seven Philippino men that now surrounded him wore rubber sandals, "flip-flops" to Ross. They also wore fairly worn-out blue jeans, white cotton T-shirts and red bandanas tied around their heads, making them all look the same, as if they were gang members, which is exactly what they were. Ross would find out later that one of them was Bhoy Santos.

Santos had lost a close friend a couple of years ago during a gunfight in which one of his own gang accidently shot and killed his boyhood friend, also a member of his gang. It had affected him deeply. To keep that from ever happening again, he had all of his gang dress alike whenever he thought there could be trouble, like another shoot-out. Today was one of those days.

As Ross was being manhandled towards the back of the jeepney that had stopped in front of him, three Philippine Constabulary armored vehicles suddenly appeared from a side street and parked on three sides of it, pinning it to the curb. With a pillowcase over his head, Ross couldn't see the Philippine Constabulary troops that quickly surrounded the gang that was in the act of kidnapping him. With over a dozen M-16s pointed at them plus the .50 caliber machine guns mounted on the tops of the armored vehicles and nowhere to run, Santos and his men meekly laid down their weapons, raised their hands and released Ross.

Just as one of the "good guys" removed the pillowcase from his head and a second one cut the duct tape that bound his wrists, a third man removed the tape that covered his mouth. Ross had never felt so relieved in his entire life. He had dreaded the thought of ending up like Lieutenant Davis.

"Sorry we took so long, Captain Ross," the PC captain facing him began, "but we had to catch them in the act of kidnapping you to make sure the charges against them would stick. With the help of the U.S. Embassy video cameras that are always filming the front gate area, we will have an easy case to prove. Thank you for helping us catch Bhoy Santos and his gang. We will keep you informed if we find out who may have killed your fellow officer."

"And thank you and your men for helping me too," Ross replied. "You got here just in time!"

He shook the PC captain's hand and then watched as the gang that had tried to kidnap him was hauled off in a specially-designed prison transport vehicle that had driven up only moments before. His heart was still racing from the perilous event.

As the last of the vehicles pulled away from the curb, Ross went back inside of the embassy compound, trying his best to look and act normal as if nothing had happened at all. The Philippine Constabulary vehicles joined the flow of traffic on busy Roxas Boulevard, now heavier than ever. Rush hour traffic in Manila was something Ross was not looking forward to driving in.

Maribel exited the main building a couple of minutes later, a big smile on her face and a new U.S. passport in her shoulder bag. She didn't have a clue about what had just happened to Ross and that was just the way he wanted it. The less she knew about the dangers his job sometimes entailed, the better, he thought.

Just as she was about to ask Ross if it had rained any while she was inside, a clap of thunder sounded in the distance and a strong breeze began to blow from the east, easing the feel of heat and humidity. Dark rain clouds now covered the sky. As if driving in heavy city traffic wasn't bad enough, now Ross had to drive in heavy rain half-way back to Clark Air Base as well, with Maribel giving him directions so he wouldn't get lost. It was a long, slow trip back to the base.

Maribel asked Ross lots of questions about his thoughts, feelings and early life experiences as they drove slowly north through the dark, wet streets of Manila, followed by Valenzuela, Bocaue, Malolos, San Fernando (Pampanga Province), Angeles City, and finally, Clark Air Base. It had stopped raining by the time they'd reached the base main gate. Off to their right, Ross noticed some Americans who lived in an off-base subdivision, filling up their large water containers with clean water at the water "filling station." They'd been told that it was safer to drink water that came from the base than the water provided by the local sources and so the water "filling station" near Clark's main gate stayed busy day and night.

His last psychoanalysis session was finally coming to an end and Ross was feeling very happy about that. He felt as if a big weight was being lifted off of him and he could finally focus entirely on his future now instead of his past. He just barely had enough time to tell Maribel that he appreciated all of her efforts in helping him, especially in the sessions that were held outside of her office, when he pulled up to the curb in front of the large white building that was the 13th Air Force Regional Medical Center.

The rain had finally stopped and the sun was about to set behind the dark mountains to the west of the base. The air smelled fresh, all the dust having been washed from it. Maribel was in good spirits too. She'd just finished her last psychoanalysis session with Ross and she was pleased with the results, both for his sake and hers. As she exited the blue government vehicle she'd spent the last few hours in, she poked her head back inside before closing the door.

"Tom, don't forget what I said. If you ever feel the need to talk about things, anything at all, give me or my dad a call."

That was the first time in Ross' memory that Maribel had referred to Doctor Edwards as "my dad."

"OK, I will. And thanks again for showing me around Manila today. I really had a good time."

Their heads were only a couple of feet away from eachother inside the car and as Ross looked in her pretty brown eyes, there was an awkward moment of silence, the kind that exists during the end of a first date when the boy is trying to decide if he should try to kiss the girl or not.

"Me too. Bye!" ended the awkward moment. Maribel turned away, closed the door and walked through the main entrance doors of the hospital that opened automatically, then disappeared from his sight.

"Yeah, I had a real good time too," he said out loud to himself, "except for being kidnapped with a hood over my head! The things I do for my country..." he sarcastically concluded as he drove off.

CHAPTER 13

July is a very hot month in the central part of the island of Luzon, where Clark Air Base is located. The rainy season as well as typhoon season had already begun in June, so humidity levels were much higher now than they had been back in February, during the dry season.
Ross had completed all of the required counseling and psychoanalysis sessions that had been stipulated as a condition to returning to duty as an AFOSI agent. Doctor Edwards had signed off on his paperwork too, satisfying Major Dickinson, the AFOSI detachment commander. Now Captain Tom Ross was once again a full-fleged member of an Air Force Office of Special Investigations unit, AFOSI Detachment 9005.
Recently, an enlisted man assigned to

the 3rd Aircraft Generation Equipment Squadron at Clark was found smoking marijuana with his Philippina girlfriend one night at one of the covered picnic pavilions near the horse riding stables on base. That recreational area was run by the Morale, Welfare and Recreation Squadron.

Clark Air Base was the largest U.S. military base in land area in the world. It even had its own aircraft gunnery range, called Crow Valley, a few miles north of the main part of the base. There, the Air Force Security Police conducted air base defense courses, teaching its troops using classroom and hands-on training, how to clear buildings with flash-bang devices and hand grenades, how to repulse attacks on the base using such weapons as 60mm and 81mm mortars, .30 and .50 caliber machine guns and a variety of other weapons and techniques.

Clark Air Base was so large that to cover most of the territory it occupied with security forces, the military police had a horse patrol unit, a motorcycle patrol unit as well as foot patrols and multi-use vehicle patrols. They also had a large dog kennel with some dogs trained to sniff out drugs and explosives. Some of their German shepherds were used to hunt down people who had climbed over a fence or wall and had gotten onto the base illegally.

In this particular case, a regular patrol car, cruising around slowly with no lights on as it drove down the dirt roads that led from one covered picnic pavilion to another, detected a couple in the area that was off-limits at night. It slowly crept up on the dating couple from behind, catching them red-handed with a lit joint as they sat on top of a picnic table, looking off in the distance. The young lady was taken to the main gate of the base and turned over to the local police and the young, stoned-out-of-his-mind airman was taken into custody. He claimed that he didn't know the area was off-limits at night when the security police asked him why he was there after dark. A big sign posted at the entrance road to the area made that fact clear to anyone bothering to read it.

While being questioned, he freely admitted to having bought the weed from another American he'd met while visiting the mountain city of Baguio, a few hours drive north of Clark Air Base. Many personnel and their families living at Clark visited Baguio to get some relief from the heat and humidity since that city was in the cooler and drier higher elevations of the mountains.

"Where did you meet this other American?" asked Tech Sergeant Winters, night shift supervisor of the Security Police Squadron.

"At a place, I think it was called the Cafe Amapola or something like that, I'm not sure. My girlfriend told me she'd been there before on a previous visit." The airman had red-rimmed eyes and looked half-asleep. He and his girlfriend were on their third joint when they were apprehended.

"And what was the person's name that sold you the bag of marijuana? Do you remember that?" the sergeant asked, putting extra emphasis on the word "that." He was starting to look a little bit angry.

"Jim something or other. I really don't remember," replied Airman First Class Alan Lumis. In his present state of mind, he couldn't remember much of anything.

"So this guy Jim, he just walks up to you and offers to sell you, a perfect stranger, a bag of marijuana, is that it?" Winters asked sarcastically. He didn't like people he called "pot heads." He didn't want them in his Air Force either.

"Yeah, sort of. I mean, my girlfriend and me, we were just sitting down eating lunch and he sits down right next to me and starts talking like he already knows me, you know? Next thing I know, he shows me a bag of weed under the table and me and my girl like to party and so I said, 'Hell yeah, let's do this,' you know?"

"If you saw this guy Jim again, would you be able to identify him?" asked the security police NCO.

"Sure, you can't miss that dude. He's got red hair and he's at least six feet tall and skinny as hell," Lumis said, smiling through eyes that were now half-closed.

Five minutes later, the First Sergeant of his squadron showed up and took custody of him. The security police section turned their report of the marijuana-smoking incident over to the local AFOSI detachment. Since a drug deal had gone down between an American GI stationed at Clark Air Base and another American in Baguio, possibly a GI stationed at nearby Camp John Hay, it was a case for the OSI to look into.

The next day, the trip to Camp John Hay that Ross had been planning for that coming weekend on his days off, had to be cancelled. He wanted to escape from the high heat and higher humidity of central Luzon and enjoy a couple of days in the cooler climate of the mountains to the north. As luck would have it, now he had to change his plans. His boss was sending him there to try and locate a tall, skinny, red-headed American who had sold some marijuana in Baguio to a GI from Clark Air Base. Maybe that might lead to a supplier or a drug dealer with a big stash or bigger connections. Catching a major player in the drug business was something every agent dreamed of, but rarely ever happened.

Ross took the business card out of his wallet and dialed the phone number on it. "Hello, Maribel? Yeah, hi! I'm afraid I've got to cancel my weekend plans for Baguio."

"Really? Why? I've already made reservations for two rooms at the Nevada Hotel. Are you not feeling well?" She was more concerned about his well-being than disappointed at the news of the cancellation.

Even though she'd volunteered to show him around the mountain city she'd visited several times before, acting as his guide and translator, she still felt, first and foremost, that she was his counselor since she'd been doing that for so long. Having gotten to know him so well over the duration of all of his sessions with her, she allowed herself to think of him as a friend too, not just a former patient. She felt that there was nothing wrong with a purely platonic relationship, based on his behavior and her ability to help him heal. She had gotten a lot of self-satisfaction from his progress, a result of her diligence as a professional soon-to-be, board-certified psychiatrist.

"I'm doing great but the Air Force has given me an assignment that will require me to be traveling and working over this weekend."

"Oh, I'm so sorry to hear that. May I ask where you're traveling to or is that confidential?" She was aware of some aspects of his profession. Some things just couldn't be discussed with anyone.

"Coincidentally, I have to go to Camp John Hay and some places in Baguio but I don't know exactly how long I'll have to be there." Then he added, "That's weird, right? I was already planning on going there anyway and letting you show me around the area and now I have to go there on official business and end up being there that same weekend."

"Yes, that's quite a coincidence all right. Well, would it still be possible if I met you at the Nevada Hotel at the time we had originally planned on and then when you have some free time, still show you around some? I hate to waste this opportunity when I'm able to go there on my own free time and already have reservations." Her voice trailed off a bit, sounding somewhat sad and disappointed to Ross.

He felt really bad for her and agreed that it would be a shame to lose this opportunity, especially for him, because she was going to be his tour guide and interpreter as well. Hey, wait a minute, he thought. I may actually need some help getting around off base up there and, who knows, maybe she can even help me find the guy I'm looking for by talking to the locals for me. Why didn't I think of that before?

"Maribel, are you still there?"

"Yes, I'm listening."

"I just had an idea. I'll fill you in on all the details later but can you get up there by yourself and meet me at the hotel at the time we originally planned?"

"Yes, that's no problem at all. But I can only stay the weekend. You said you didn't know how long you may have to stay there?"

"Yes, that's right. After you leave, I'll just stay on the base. I'm sure I can find some 'down time' from work so you can show me around some. Things might still work out somehow. See you there then?"

"Yes, I'll be there. Bye now," she said, in a very cheery voice, happy to still be going there after all. She had been enjoying herself while showing Ross historic sites and explaining the history of the country to him, using the information she'd gained from her classes at the University of the Philippines and her own personal experiences while traveling to many of these locations with her parents.

With that plan in place, Ross felt some relief. The idea of going to Baguio, a place he'd never been to before, and finding a drug dealer, even one who stuck out in a crowd, presented some challenges. But now, it would be much easier since Maribel would be with him. She knew the town, spoke the language and she knew him as well as anyone ever did, so he wouldn't be with a stranger. The local dialect spoken in Baguio wasn't the Tagalog that Maribel knew so well but a lot of people in Baguio could also speak Tagalog and that would still be very helpful to Ross.

In regards to Maribel being in Baguio with him, Ross felt that he knew her and her family too, at least to some extent. Somehow, he found comfort in that. Maribel Edwards had helped him recover psychologically and she could help him while he did his job as an OSI agent too. That gave him yet another reason to like her. He was beginning to feel like she was more than just a "shrink" and a good tour guide. Now she was also a friend. After everything he'd been through over the past few years, he could use another friend.


The first part of the trip from Clark Air Base to Baguio was very slow-going for Ross. After driving through the main gate of the base, he had to drive the government vehicle through a small portion of Angeles City to reach MacArthur Highway. Large open fields were on his left with a mixture of bars and sari-sari stores on his left on the other side of the open fields. He could see the backs of the wall-to-wall bars on Fields Avenue to his right as he headed towards the busy two-lane highway. That's when he hit lots of traffic, just after turning left onto one of the main roads in the country, and one of the busiest.

Time after time he had to step on the brake pedal as jeepneys or tricycles, which were motorcycles with covered sidecars attached, slowed down in front of him to turn off the road to pick up or let off passengers. There were no lines painted in the center of the road, so a person could pass another vehicle just about anywhere they wanted to but oncoming traffic kept Ross in his lane until he was well out of town.

The land between Angeles City and the river bridge near Bamban to the north was very flat. There were sugar cane fields and rice paddies on both sides of the road in this area as the predominant landscape features he saw. Every once in a while he would see a two-and-a-half ton logging truck with long sugar cane stalks piled so high, he couldn't understand how they ever made it under electric wires or not break down from being overloaded. Far off to the west, he could see the Zambales Mountains with very high peaks like that of Mount Tapulo, which was 2,037 meters high. In comparison, Mount Pinatubo, which was much closer to Angeles City, was only 1,450 meters in height.

The road gradually rose in elevation and the land began to become hilly between Bamban and Capas. He slowed down as he neared the stone markers and sign which pointed to Camp O'Donnell, a short distance west of the highway. After the fall of the Bataan Peninsula in early 1942, the Japanese took their prisoners here, those that survived the brutal and infamous Bataan Death March that is. He couldn't see the camp from the road, only dry open fields, gently sloping downward from the west side of the highway.

While driving in-between some towns, Ross was able to pick up speed as the traffic thinned out, getting up to 60 miles per hour sometimes. Then, on the outskirts of Rosario, the road forked. It made him think of the funny quote by the famous New York Yankee's catcher, Yogi Berra, "If you come to a fork in the road, take it." In this case, he remembered to take the right fork. There was a sign posted there, pointing the way to Baguio, even if he'd forgotten which fork to take.

Had he taken the left one, he'd have ended up in Damortis, next to the Lingayen Gulf. A right turn in Damortis, going north along National Highway, and he would have found Wallace Air Station, another American military installation, near the town of San Fernando in La Union Province. He would have had to turn left off the National Highway just south of San Fernando and then he would have seen that Wallace Air Station was on a narrow peninsula called Poro Point, jutting out into the South China Sea. It was one of the most beautiful, scenic places that an American military member could be stationed at in the Philippines.

Two passenger buses passed him shortly before the highway started angling steeply upward, looking as if they were in a race to see who would reach Baguio first. One of them had the name PANTRANCO on it and the other, PHILIPPINE RABBIT. Both were spewing out dark clouds of smelly diesel exhaust and Ross noticed that every window on both buses were wide open. Only the expensive tour buses around Manila seemed to be air conditioned.

Once the highway began zig-zagging near a river and getting progressively steeper, Ross began to get worried. There were many steep drop-offs from very high elevations down to rock and boulder-strewn riverbanks far below, and there were no guardrails to keep anyone from going over the side to a certain death. He couldn't imagine anyone surviving a crash in a bus, rolling and tumbling down a steep mountain side.

He passed slowly by a huge, carved-in-stone, lion's head near a hair-pin turn in the road and marveled at how life-like it looked. It was located on one of the steepest parts of the road and all of the traffic slowed down a lot in this section of it. He finally passed by a bus station with a very large parking lot on the side of the road and then the steep climb was over. Baguio at last! He'd traveled almost one hundred miles from Clark Air Base to the city of Baguio but it had seemed much farther because of the zig-zag mountain road that contained many switchbacks in the steep hill sides.

The first place that Ross and Maribel went to after checking into separate rooms at the Nevada Hotel was Cafe Amapola. Large green awnings hung over the two big windows facing the street of the popular restaurant and bar. It had been the location of the drug deal between two Americans that resulted in Ross being sent here. He was hoping the seller of the marijuana would return again while he was present. The multi-story building appeared to house some apartments above the ground floor business establishment. The food served here was very good and that's why the place was full of diners when Ross and Maribel arrived.

As soon as they sat down, Ross looked

around the dining room but didn't see anyone
fitting the description of the person he was
looking for. Red hair would have stood out
like a neon light at night in this room full
of dark-haired diners. He scanned the menu
given to him by a smiling young female waitress and he knew right away that he was going to need some help making up his mind.
There were just too many good things to
choose from.

Maribel was sitting across from him at a
small table they'd been led to near the back
wall of the restaurant. It had been one of
the last empty tables available. She looked
up from her menu and asked, "Find anything
you like?"

She was wearing a blue, long sleeve
blouse under a white sweater, blue jeans,
white socks and white tennis shoes. The
weather here was a lot cooler and drier than
at Clark Air Base, and the lack of humidity
was very noticeable too. Outdoors, a lot of
the locals wore sweaters and jackets year-
round.

Ross also wore blue jeans, but a little
more worn than hers were, along with his
favorite tan belt with a large silver buckle
and matching tan boots. He'd chosen a gray
sweatshirt over a white T-shirt to stay
warm. Looking around again, he noticed the
other diners were dressed casually as well.

"Except for the chicken fried rice, I
don't know what else I want. Do you want to
split something, maybe choose a couple of
things and we'll just share it, kind of like
family-style?" He'd seen the large portions
most restaurants served and he liked a lot
of different things on the menu but didn't
want to eat a lot, at least not on a day
when he was going to do a lot of walking.
This town had many hills to walk up and down.

"What kinds of things do you like?" she

asked, looking up at him over the top of the plastic-covered, multi-paged menu. There were dozens upon dozens of choices to choose from, including American hot dogs.

"Well, I liked the noodles and spring rolls I've had before."

"The pancit and lumpia, you mean?"

"Yeah, and the lumpia with pork inside was really good."

"OK, I'll order us the chicken fried rice, pancit and pork lumpia then and we can split it. Anything to drink?"

He thought about having a cold San Miguel beer or a serbesa negra but decided he'd better stick to something non-alcoholic since he'd be driving again soon. "I'll just have some ice tea. That should do it, I think. Is that all right with you, the food I mean?"

"Sure. I'll also have some ice tea." She gave their order to the waitress in Tagalog and then turned her attention back to the menu.

"Have you ever tried eating balut?" she asked, hiding her smile behind the menu she held up high so that Ross could only see her face from her eyes up. Maribel knew that most Americans had never eaten one, and that included her.

"Oh, gosh no! I've seen people eat those big duck eggs, poking a hole in the top and then sucking out the juice. Then they peeled off the shell about half-way down and I saw the baby duck inside. I just couldn't understand how they could pinch off a wing or some other part and eat its' body like that. Yuk!" he said, making a face of pure disgust.

Maribel tried to hide her giggle behind the menu. All Ross could see was her eyes and he thought for the first time, while not being able to see the rest of her face, what pretty brown eyes she had. She wore no make-up, so what he saw was all natural. Then he had a quick memory flashback and saw Genevieve's half-French, half-Vietnamese brown eyes. They were so similar that it was as if it was Genevieve's eyes he was looking at now and not Maribel's. They were not quite almond-shaped, not quite round, somehow a little of both in a shape that Ross found rather intriguing.

"Why are you looking at me like that?" Maribel asked, as she lowered her menu. "You look like you just saw a ghost or something. Are you OK?"

"Oh, I'm sorry. I didn't mean to stare. I guess my mind just wandered a bit, kind of like daydreaming, you know?" He shrugged it off and smiled and then after a second or two, she smile back at him. I hope she doesn't think I need more counseling, he thought. That's the last thing I need right now.

While they ate, Ross filled Maribel in on why he was sent to Baguio and Camp John Hay and since his mission wasn't classified in any way, he could speak freely about it. He assured her that it was not a dangerous case he was dealing with, so she had nothing to worry about in case they happened to cross paths with the tall red-headed man he was looking for.

Afterwards, they had just enough time to take a drive to Burnham Park before it got dark. They left the government motorpool car that Ross had driven up from Clark Air Base in, parked at one end of Burnham Park, then they took a leisurely walk. They began a slow pace around the boating lagoon, walking between Luna Drive, Lake Drive and Abad Santos. Several couples had rented flat-bottom boats with elevated roofs on them and some couples were in smaller canoes and paddle boats that you powered with your feet, pedaling like a bicycle to propel them through the water.

Watching other couples walking hand-in-hand or cuddling while out on the small lake as he and Maribel strolled leisurely along, made Ross feel a little envious. He missed that in life, holding Genevieve's soft hands and holding her close to him. He knew that he had to get beyond the past and move on but it was not easy for him to do so. Not yet anyway.

Genevieve had once explained how she was Buddhist, Confucianist and Catholic all at the same time and Ross knew that some Buddhists believed in reincarnation. That could mean either a person dies and then is reborn in a new form or body or that their soul alone is reborn in a new human body. Had Genevieve somehow been reincarnated and that was why he sometimes saw some of her physical characteristics in Maribel? No, he told himself, that's just crazy. It can't be. Maybe his brain was just playing tricks on him. Let it go...

Maribel broke the silence as they walked back to the car and put an end to Ross' self-talk in his mind. "I have a few places to show you when you have time tomorrow. This park is just one of many nice things to see here in Baguio. For example, we can go to Mine's View Park and watch silversmiths make beautiful jewelry from the silver that's mined not far from here and also that park has some lookout points where you can see some places that are several miles away on other mountains or down below in valleys. Not far from here is the beautiful Baguio Buddhist Temple and the St. Louis University Museum. We could even stop by the president's summer residence and see what a beautiful house he has. We can't go on the grounds but we could take some pictures from the park across the street from there."

The sun was about to disappear behind a mountain and the chill in the air was becoming more noticeable as Ross and Maribel drove back to their hotel. "Yeah, that sounds great," he said. "I'll knock on your door as soon as I get a chance to take a break tomorrow. Tell you what. I'll just take an extra-long lunch break and pick you up at noon. How's that sound?"

"That sounds great. I think you'll enjoy seeing the sights here. There's so much to see and do around Baguio."

"I know one thing I'm enjoying already. Care to guess what it is?" he teased. He was enjoying her company but he wasn't going to tell her that. The impish smile he now displayed made him look a few years younger, in Maribel's eyes.

She rolled her eyes, put an index finger up to her cheek and looked up at the darkening sky and said, "Hmmm, let's see now. The cool mountain air?" she asked, hoping he'd say it was her company instead.

"Very good!" he exclaimed with a laugh. "Now let's get inside where it's warmer," he said, as he parked the car.

You're such a tease, Tom Ross, Maribel thought to herself as they said goodnight and headed for separate rooms. It was the last peaceful night the city of Baguio would have for a very long time.

## CHAPTER 14

The next day, July 16th, Ross drove the short distance from the Nevada Hotel to Camp John Hay. The hotel was conveniently located near the main entrance to the base. The U.S. military R & R facility was approximately six hundred and seven acres in size, a true mountain resort get-a-way for those seeking relief from the heat of the lowlands. There were cabins to rent, a well-manicured golf course to play on, a gym to exercise in and places to eat. It also had beautiful scenery like the Fil-Am Friendship Garden near the Main Club and the award-winning Ifugao garden which was built by Department of Defense Security Policemen, all native Philippinos, on a center island on the main road.

Ross had two things to do on the base

that morning. The first was to make lodging reservations for himself since Maribel would be returning to Clark Air Base the next day and their reservations at the Nevada Hotel were only for that weekend and he would be staying longer. The second thing was to check in with Master Sergeant Ron Thatcher, Chief, Security Police, to see if his department could help him locate the tall, skinny red-headed drug dealer who was thought to be stationed here. The Master Sergeant was out on patrol with a new member of their organization and wouldn't be back for a while so Ross decided to return later.

He'd never been to Camp John Hay before and he was pleasantly surprised by how beautiful the place looked. The cool, dry, clean mountain air had a pine scent to it as pine trees greatly outnumbered the other types. There wasn't a cloud in the sky and Ross decided to take advantage of the nice weather and take a ride around the base before heading back to Baguio.

As he slowly drove down Sheridan Drive, Country Club Road, Lawton Road and Ordonio Drive, he marveled at the cleanliness of the grounds and well-kept buildings that were mostly painted white with green trim. He passed by the two-story gym at a leisurely twenty miles per hour and was surprised to see tall chimneys rising up from both ends. It was obviously a very old, but well-kept structure, also painted white with green trim. Well-manicured lawns, flower beds and trimmed shrubs seemed to be everywhere. This was definitely not your average military base. Plus, it also surprised him at how very little traffic there was.

By the time he got back to the Nevada Hotel, it was almost noon. He had only a few minutes to go to his room and get his camera before meeting with Maribel. He parked the blue government sedan near the left corner of the building, below his third floor room, which was directly above it at the end of the hall.

Ross was in a good mood and decided to stop at Maribel's room which was also on the third floor, three doors down from his. It wasn't noon yet, but what the heck, it would be soon and since he'd have to walk by her room to get to his, well, that made his decision an easy one.

The door opened slowly after the third knock.

"Hello, Tom," Maribel said, as she leaned over and slipped on her other shoe. "You're a couple of minutes early."

"I just have to grab my camera from my room and I'll be ready to go do some sightseeing. Since I had to pass by your door on the way there, well, I just had to stop and say 'hi.' Be back in a minute." They were both smiling and looking happy and eager to get going.

"OK," she replied in a cheerful tone. "I'll just get my shoulder bag and wait for you here."

He turned and walked quickly down the well-lit, deserted hall. It was lined with brightly-colored floral paintings on both sides. Ross had left his camera in the black suitcase he'd placed on a chair between his queen size bed and the far wall that had a large window that overlooked the front parking lot. As he reached into the suitcase, he heard a loud noise, almost like the BOOM of an explosion, then he was suddenly and violently knocked off his feet. The floor fell out from under him as the entire building collapsed onto the first floor and shook ferociously back and forth. Before he could even try to get back on his feet, the building shook violently again and a strong rumbling sound filled his ears. As the whole room continued to shake, the large cabinet containing a big heavy TV, several drawers for clothes and a clock radio, fell on top of him, knocking him out cold. At that moment he'd been on his hands and knees on the carpeted floor, trying to make some sense of what was happening. He never saw the cabinet falling over.

The scene was even worse in Maribel's room just a short distance down the hall. She'd been in the bathroom, looking in the mirror over the sink. When the first floor of the building disappeared into the ground with the rest of it partially pancaked on top, she was knocked off her feet and fell onto her left side on the cold tile floor, facing away from the outer wall. She also heard the same loud booming sound that Ross had heard. She knew immediately that it was an earthquake. This wasn't her first one, though it would be, by far, the worst.

As Maribel attempted to sit up from her prone position, the entire outside wall of the bathroom, containing the large mirrored medicine cabinet and heavy porcelain sink and its plumbing, came crashing down on top of her. She felt a quick stab of pain and then she was knocked unconscious.

The cement balcony wall on a second floor room was now on top of the blue government motorpool car that Ross had driven up from Clark Air Base. The engine compartment and roof were both crushed flat by tons of cement. Several other vehicles that had been parked in a row next to the heavily damaged hotel were also damaged beyond repair, with parts of the Nevada Hotel on top of them.

Over a dozen people on the first floor of the hotel were crushed to death during the first major jolt of what seismologists described as a major 7.9 earthquake. On the

Richter scale, which is an open-ended logarithmic scale for measuring the magnitude of an earthquake in terms of the energy dissipated in it, a 1.5 would be the smallest earthquake that can be felt and a 4.5 earthquake normally caused only slight damage. On this day, the powerful 7.9 earthquake that struck the mountainous northern part of the island of Luzon, caused catastrophic devastation and many deaths, especially in and around the mountain city of Baguio.

    Almost one hundred miles to the south, at Clark Air Base, several witnesses reported seeing the solid ground in their yards on base roll like ocean waves as their vehicles bounced up and down in their driveways or in parking lots. Cabinet doors flew open in many apartments, duplexes and houses in the various base housing areas. A couple of water pipes burst and several buildings developed cracks in their walls but there were no deaths and only a few minor injuries reported.

    Around Baguio, people weren't so lucky. On Camp John Hay, even the base commander had a close call. One of the two chimneys that stuck out of the roof of his residence toppled over and left a gaping hole in the structure. Luckily, neither he nor anyone in his family were injured.

    One of the two chimneys on the old base gym buckled, damaging one of the end walls very badly. The stucco facade on the streetside of the Mountain Breeze Recreation Center cracked from the roof all the way down to the foundation. There were many aftershocks and with each one, the damage just continued to get worse.

    At cottage number 113, which was one of the VIP quarters, the strong earthquake knocked it completely from its foundation. After four more days of strong aftershocks, one corner room separated completely from the rest of the building and the chimney was leaning over with roof damage around it.

One family that lived in Military Family Housing had to move out of their house because it was knocked off of its foundation and walls and floors buckled badly in many places. Fortunately, no one inside was seriously injured. Many of the buildings on Camp John Hay had fireplaces and also hot water heaters that were located on the outside of the structures, up against the sides somewhere. More than fifty 50-gallon hot water heaters were destroyed when the powerful earthquake knocked them down.

The warehouse used to store softdrinks and beer remained standing but thousands of glass bottles and many cans lost their liquid contents when the earthquake toppled stacks of sodas and beer all over the floor of the building.

There were many places along the main roads on base where the sidewalks buckled and stuck up at strange angles. Many of the chimneys still standing after the earthquake and strong aftershocks had to be pulled down to prevent any further damage to the buildings because of their weakened condition.

There were eight major water main breaks and many smaller breaks and leaks scattered across Camp John Hay. The power was knocked out because several transformers were shaken from their power poles. It would take several days before water service was restored and everyone on base had electricity again. Luckily no one on Camp John Hay died that day but less than a mile away, there were many deaths and injuries.

Within a minute to a minute-and-a-half, the once beautiful city of Baguio was devastated. Huge clouds of dust filled the air as dozens of large buildings collapsed or fell apart. People couldn't run out into the streets from the buildings they were in because the buildings and the ground on which they stood, shook too much. Most people couldn't even remain standing where they were when the severe shaking and ground-rolling began.

In the Chinese Park at the foot of Session Road, a popular tourist destination, one steep-roofed building broke into pieces, with one section of it crushing and decapitating a female vendor who worked there and sold drinks and snacks to tourists. Portions of the University of Baguio commerce building collapsed and many students died that day, unable to leave the six-story building in time.

The whole area to the left of St. Vincent Catholic church along the Naguilian Road sank almost three-and-a-half feet. Part of the hillside next to the double-steepled church caved in and formed a small landslide along the side of the road.

Golfers on the number seven fairway on the Camp John Hay golf course watched in astonishment and horror as the nearby ten-story tall Hyatt Hotel trembled, shook, then fell over to one side, a near-total collapse that killed dozens of people. Only one portion of the building remained standing, though heavily damaged. A few minutes after the dust settled, a few hotel patrons tied bedsheets together and made their way down the outside of the building that was left standing. They left their rooms that way after discovering it was their only way out of the tall structure after stairwells collapsed and elevators were without power. For some, it was a long and dangerous climb down.

The FRB Hotel, located near the University of Baguio commerce building, also collapsed, killing a dozen people inside, guests as well as employees. When the Royal Inn, located along Magsaysay Avenue on the north side of town collapsed, it took on a strange tilt towards the road. The entire first floor was crushed flat with no survivors and dozens of people, mostly employees, died instantly.

Not far from there, near the intersection of Hilltop Road and Magsaysay Avenue, the Baguio Hilltop Hotel crumbled into pieces. Tons of debris covered the dead and a few survivors. Cries of "Help! Help us!" could be heard everywhere in the streets of Baguio all day long.

On Harrison Road and within easy walking distance to the Burnham Park boating lagoon stood the seven-story tall Burnham Park Hotel. The six people walking down the street that went along the side of it were all crushed to death when the hotel completely collapsed and covered that street with tons of heavy building materials. It was one of the most completely destroyed buildings in all of Baguio. Every floor collapsed down on the one below it and then the entire death-trap fell over to one side, killing even more people outside of the building. Dozens of people were crushed to death in the collapse of the once-beautiful hotel.

The three-story Crown Victoria Hotel suffered severe damage and a car that was parked near the front door was totally demolished when part of the building fell on it, killing the driver and one passenger inside.

The Baguio Colleges Foundation building and a commercial factory on Ferguson Road were also severly damaged, injuring dozens of people at both locations but miraculously no deaths were reported from either place.

Eight people were killed inside the Cafe Amapola where Ross and Maribel had eaten just the day before. Both large front windows were broken out and the second floor collapsed into the first floor, sending ceiling fans, light fixtures and building materials onto the unlucky diners, cooks and waitresses. One of the diners was a teenage college student, a local girl. Her companion was a tall, skinny, young American male with red hair. They were crushed to death, dying instantly.

The Baguio Country Club was just across the street from the east side of Camp John Hay, along Country Club Road. It was a well-built, six-story tall structure and it suffered major damage when the second floor collapsed down onto the first floor. Luckily for those people on the higher floors, they didn't pancake down, one on top of the other like some of the other hotels had done that day. For those people crushed to death on the first floor, their luck had run out.

Besides the initial 7.9 magnitude earthquake, many strong aftershocks began soon afterwards. Some of the buildings that had not collapsed right away did later on and those that didn't, like the Skyworld building downtown, was so badly damaged and leaning that it and others had to be demolished at a later date.

Baguio also suffered major damage to many sidewalks that had large cracks in them and large cracks also appeared in the earth in many places. Many roads also became impassable because of landslides and large cracks in the surface.

Some of the worst damage around Baguio occurred at the Philippine Military Academy, especially to the enlisted staff housing area. Many buildings were totally destroyed and many more were damaged beyond repair. Several deaths were reported there, of men, women and children.

Many power lines were knocked down, as well as telephone lines. In one section of Baguio, people stood in long lines for several hours just to place a phone call on one of the very few phones that still worked.

Some of the area hospitals had been so badly damaged by the earthquake that patients had to be moved outdoors. All newly-injured patients were seen and treated outside. The fear was, some of those powerful aftershocks might bring down buildings that were already damaged, especially buildings used by the University of the Philippines on Govenor Center Road and Govenor Pack Road and the University of Baguio. Students from both universities were told to evacuate all buildings and go home. The next day, hundreds of students could be seen walking down the Naguilian Road past the devastated city of Baguio, headed for a bus station or for some, a long walk home. Those were the lucky ones. Hundreds of their fellow college students didn't survive the strongest earthquake in modern times to hit this mountainous area.

Panic set in when the earthquake began, especially after people discovered that walking, much less running, was almost impossible because of the ground or building shaking and rolling so much. Earthquakes were as common on the large island of Luzon as they were in Japan or California but they had never experienced one this strong before. It had been incredibly powerful and destructive.

People could be heard screaming during and after the earthquake. Most of the screams heard afterwards were from those who had been injured, trapped in the rubble, or both. A few screams occurred when someone uninjured went back into a damaged building only to find the person or people they were searching for, squashed like a bug by heavy objects and/or building materials.

The 7.9 earthquake had not only been very intense but had lasted much longer than the average earthquake. To make matters even worse, the many aftershocks themselves were sometimes as strong as a medium-intensity earthquake and caused even more death and destruction for weeks afterwards. For example, three strong aftershocks hit the area on the morning of August 9th and caused more damage and rattled the nerves of those who had lived through the initial destruction back on July 16th. Buildings damaged by the initial earthquake sometimes sank deeper into the ground or broke apart even more, killing and injuring more people. To some survivors who were interviewed by the media people who showed up several days later, it seemed like the end of the world was happening.

Point-to-point communications were eventually made and word got out to other towns, cities and military bases about the catastrophe that had occurred in and around Baguio. The first emergency responders were overwhelmed by the immensity of the situation. Some of them had to try and rescue and save the lives of some of their co-workers where they worked before being able to move into surrounding areas. Others found themselves in need of being rescued, being buried under buildings that had fallen apart. Some of their rescue equipment had been damaged and even some of their vehicles were now useless piles of junk, crushed by collapsed buildings.

Those fire department and local police personnel that were able to help others soon found themselves with a monumental task at hand. So many buildings had been severly damaged and destroyed and so many people were calling out for help. Where do you begin? Many unknown heroes that day were simply average people, caught up in a once-in-a-lifetime cataclysmic event that would change many lives forever.

One such hero remained anonymous because of his shady past. The thirty-seven year old man had been arrested many times over the past ten years for theft. The local man refused to give his name to anyone who asked because he knew the police were still looking for him for another crime he committed, stealing again. He led a life of crime but yet, when the powerful earthquake knocked him to his knees as he walked near a hotel at the edge of town, the screams he heard coming from within the collapsed building, tore at his heart. He may not have been a law-abiding citizen but he was a human being and could not turn away.

He couldn't see the person who was doing the screaming but he thought the female voice was coming from one of the upper floors of the hotel. He looked around at the heavily damaged building, trying to find a way in. The entrance doors on the ground floor had been pancaked under the second floor and he tried to find another way into the building.

He looked across the street and saw a truck with a six-foot-long wooden ladder tied to the top. The door of the panel truck had the name of a company that was in the house painting business. Perfect! He was only going to borrow the ladder, not steal it this time. He carried it over to the corner of the hotel where he leaned the top of it against the third floor balcony of someone's room. It just happened to be an area that was now closest to the ground. The balcony door was either locked or jammed shut but since the window was broken out, he gingerly climbed over the window sill, careful not to touch any of the jagged pieces of glass sticking up around the edges of the window frame. This had been the only way he could get inside of the building in order to help whoever it was that had been screaming. He stopped moving for a second to listen, but the screaming had now stopped. After not hearing anything, he decided to make his way to the central hallway through this room he was in.

    To reach the door leading to the hallway, the man had to walk around a large cabinet that had fallen over. As he made his way to the door, he looked down behind him to get a second look at what he thought was a human leg but wasn't completely sure. He turned and retraced his steps back to the dark wood cabinet. It was a leg!

    It took the man several attempts to move the heavy cabinet but with a super-human, adrenaline-charged effort, he got it off of the prostrated form that had been covered up beneath it. Then he removed the large heavy television that was resting in the center of the man's back. The electricity was off but there was enough light coming in through the large window to see in the room fairly well.

    He put the back of his hand next to the nostrils of the still figure and felt the movement of air going out against the hairs on the back of his hand. He was still alive and breathing! He was afraid to move the man, thinking that he may have suffered a broken back from the heavy television and cabinet that had been on top of him.

    Then, instinctively, he removed the man's wallet from his back pocket. Once a thief, always a thief. He found some green American dollars and a few Philippine peso bills and suddenly realized this guy must be an American. The Philippinos he knew would never keep American dollars. If they ever got some, they'd immediately change them to pesos with a black market money-changer and make a good profit over the legal exchange rate.

Then he did something very unusual for him. After looking the bills over, he returned them all to the wallet. He felt sorry for the injured guy, laying there unconscious on the floor. Then he looked for some form of identification, curious as to who this person was. He quickly found a laminated card that had UNITED STATES UNIFORMED SERVICES printed at the top and a photo and name, along with a signature under it. The man he'd discovered was Captain Tom Ross, U.S. Air Force.

An idea suddenly popped into his head. Even though the screaming he'd heard before had stopped, maybe there still could be others needing help too, buried under rubble like this man had been, in this heavily-damaged hotel. He must hurry and get help for this guy fast, while he was still alive, because there might still be others alive as well. The room began shaking as an aftershock struck the area and this soon-to-be hero became very scared of becoming injured or trapped himself. He took one last look at the injured man on the floor and quickly headed back outside for the ladder.

He knew this building was what was left of the Nevada Hotel, even though the sign that used to be on the front was no longer there anymore. He was no stranger to this neighborhood. Once back on the ground, he jogged over to the main entrance to Camp John Hay to report the finding of a seriously injured American. It wasn't very far from the hotel and he was soon there.

The man spoke to the Philippino Department of Defense security guard in their local dialect. He was almost out of breath, not used to jogging at all.

"I need some help. The Nevada Hotel collapsed and I found a badly injured American Air Force Captain inside. Can you help me?"

"I will get you some help," responded the security guard, then explained in English to the American Air Force security policeman standing next to him what had been said. Sergeant Roberto Munar had worked as a DOD security guard for a little over a year now and liked working with the Americans on Camp John Hay.

Sergeant Johnny Ruiz, the Air Force security policeman, listened intently, then said, "Tell this man, 'thank you' and to wait here. I'll be back soon with some help."

Ruiz then got into the blue Jeep Wagoneer, turned on the colored light bar mounted on the roof and the loud siren as well, then took off with squeeling tires, headed for the base infirmary. It wasn't a full-fledged hospital like Baguio General or Notre Dame Hospital but for the time being, it would have to do. At least some medical personnel were there and it was a lot closer than any of the hospitals in town.

When the anonymous man led the rescue team back to the room where he'd found Ross, he was astonished to see a message written on a small piece of paper in the injured man's right hand. He didn't remember seeing it before. Unknown to him, while he'd been gone, Ross had gained consciousness for a brief amount of time. He'd taken the slip of paper out of his pants pocket, on which he'd written two days before: Maribel Edwards Nevada Hotel Room 307. Ross hoped that she was OK and wanted anyone who found him to go and look for her. Then everything turned black again. His body was badly bruised and broken but he was not able to feel any pain.

His plan worked. After the men got him loaded into the Air Force ambulance, they went back up the ladder, through his room and down the darkened hallway to room 307. It was on the opposite side of the hall from Ross' room. The door had to be taken off the hinges and knocked down with strong shoulders for the rescue team to get in.

The first person to discover Maribel was again, the man who wished to remain anonymous. He called out to the others and then lifted the sink and wall tiles off of her before the others arrived to help. Just as he started to lean over and put an ear to her heart to see if he could detect a heartbeat, a medic put a stethoscope to her chest and beat him to it. Then the medic felt for a pulse. She was covered in white dust so nobody could see her many bruises, only the blood trickling from her nose and both ears.

"She's still alive, but just barely. Her pulse is very weak. We've got to hurry and get her out of here. Get the front door and put it down close to her and we'll use it for a stretcher," the ranking medic instructed, taking charge of the situation.

The other men moved quickly at the medic's command, including the man who'd found her in all the rubble. And that's how Maribel Edwards was removed from her room and the demolished Nevada Hotel, on a door carried by three Americans and one anonymous Philippino hero, who risked his life and later found and helped rescue several other lucky survivors in the Nevada Hotel before the day was over. It was for him, a day of redemption.

CHAPTER 15

Outside help was badly needed by the survivors of the deadly earthquake that devastated Baguio and the surrounding areas. Many dead and injured Americans needed to be transported to Clark Air Base where there was an excellent regional medical center and a modern mortuary facility. Roads would have to be repaired and the electrical and water systems as well. Rescue efforts to look for survivors in all the hundreds of damaged buildings would have to be done soon. This was, after all, the rainy season. Heavy rains could easily cause landslides in areas that already suffered damage from previous landslides caused by the earthquake and interfere with aircraft trying to fly in medical supplies, food and rescuers.
 Calls went out to the Philippine govern-

ment and the American military establishment and not only in this country but in neighboring countries also. The U.S. Embassy in Manila got involved in the relief effort by contacting some organizations in the United States. In no time it all, it seemed, they prepared for the long flight that would take them half-way around the world.

Helicopters of both the U.S. military forces and the Philippine Air Force began flying missions to the area, landing at Loakan Airport near Baguio and even on some of the golf course fairways at Camp John Hay. It eventually became one of the largest airlift operations since the Berlin Airlift after the end of World War II.

The local Department of Public Works and Highways, with the assistance of a Clark Air Base unit, the 3rd Civil Engineering Squadron Prime Beef team, made repairs to the badly damaged parking ramp and runway at Loakan Airport. Afterwards, U.S. Air Force C-130 Hercules cargo planes and assorted other types of smaller American and Philippine aircraft were able to land, three days after the earthquake. They brought in much-needed medical supplies, food, water and more relief workers. On their outbound flights, U.S. Air Force aircraft evacuated over 2,500 people. The C-130s also carried 38 human remains back to Clark Air Base. The death toll continued to rise as each devastated building was thoroughly searched.

The big C-130 transports flew in members of Clark's 8th Mobile Aerial Port Squadron and their big 10k (AT) All-Terrain forklifts. This hard-working unit loaded and unloaded over 190 C-130s at both Loakan and San Fernando, La Union airfields. Because the only road out of Loakan Airport was partially destroyed by sinking and also by landslides during the earthquake, smaller trucks had to be used to move cargo from the airport to Camp John Hay, transporting only one cargo pallet at a time.

A lot of the helicopters that showed up on the golf course at Camp John Hay took some evacuees down the mountain where they could get bus transportation to their destinations. Kennon Road, used by many large and small bus companies to transport people to and from Baguio every day, had become impassable due to multiple landslides.

Meanwhile, in the 13th Air Force Regional Medical Center Intensive Care Unit at Clark Air Base, Doctor Melvin Edwards sat in a plain metal-framed chair pulled up close to a patient's bed. The curtains that could be pulled completely around the bed for privacy were now closed and he was alone with his seriously-injured daughter, Maribel.

She was hooked up to several different monitors and an intravenous drip. An oxygen mask covered most of her discolored face, which included two black eyes. There was a lot of plum-purple color mixed in with the black and, in short, she looked really horrible, just lucky to be alive at this point.

A nurse walked into the room, opened the privacy curtain and said, "Oh! I didn't know you were here, Doctor Edwards." By now, everyone working in the ICU knew who he was. "How are you holding up?"

"As well as could be expected, I guess," he replied in a low voice. His face was haggard and sad-looking. The dark lines under his eyes were clear evidence that he had not slept much lately. "So, how is Maribel doing? Any changes yet?"

After checking over the machines that Maribel was connected to and the charts that were in the nurse's hands, the reply was not what he'd been hoping for. "No sir, not yet anyway. Her injuries will take a while to heal and recovery will take time but I'm sure she'll pull through OK. She's young and healthy and that counts for a lot you know."

"In other words, it's in God's hands," he sarcastically stated, followed by, "I'm sorry. I didn't mean that. I know you all are doing everything possible to help my daughter and I'm very grateful." He felt really bad now for letting his thoughts slip out.

"It's OK. You really should go home and get some sleep, Doctor Edwards. You wouldn't want Maribel to wake up and see you looking so tired and worn-out and in need of a shave, would you?"

"No, you're right. I wouldn't," he agreed. "This is the hardest part of being a parent, you know? I just hate not being here all the time. I want to be here when she opens her eyes and wakes up again."

"If you're not here when that happens, I promise I'll call you," the nurse said kindly, trying to make him feel better.

"OK. I'll go home as soon as you're finished here. How's our former patient, Captain Ross?" He was thinking about visiting him sometime soon.

"All I know is, he's also in the ICU. He's not my patient but I've heard he got injured pretty badly as well and will probably be in the hospital recovering for some time," the nurse concluded.

The two of them left the room together as Maribel Edwards clung to life by a thread. She was in worse condition than her father thought. She had a bruised skull, a concussion, several broken ribs and bruises all over her body. In laymen's terms, she was in pretty bad shape, in very serious, bordering on critical condition.

As major recovery efforts continued in Baguio after the earthquake that now made headline news around the world, more aftershocks struck the area, causing even more people to leave and seek shelter elsewhere.
The 31st Air Rescue and Recovery Squadron from Clark Air Base flew over 140 missions to Camp John Hay in their CH-3E and HH-3E helicopters over the next couple of weeks. They flew in hundreds of thousands of dollars worth of medical supplies and on the return trip, brought out many evacuees, including critically and seriously injured patients like Maribel Edwards and Air Force Captain Tom Ross.
Smaller helicopters from Clark Air Base like UH-1 "Hueys," flew around 50 missions and brought in medical personnel and at least 650 units of whole blood donated by Americans at Clark Air Base and other American bases in Asia.
The U.S. Air Force was not alone in flying American aircraft relief missions to devastated Baguio and Camp John Hay. U.S. Marine CH-53 "Jolly Green Giant" helicopters flew over 120 missions, most landing on the golf course at Camp John Hay. They flew in many tons of supplies that were badly needed like food, water and medicine. Unfortunately, two of them clipped some nearby trees when departing and had to make emergency landings. Nobody was injured in either unfortunate accident except for the pilot's pride and both choppers required blade changes before they were able to fly again.
The golf course at Camp John Hay took on the look of a military exercise as thousands

of pounds of bagged rice and other commodities were stacked along the edges of the grass between the number 9 and number 14 fairways. The Marines also operated some CH-46s which, in addition to carrying cargo and personnel in the cargo compartment, also carried sling loads of even more cargo hanging below them, just as they had done in Vietnam not all that long ago.

The damage that had been done to Camp John Hay was so extensive, more outside assistance was needed to help with the repairs. The 554th Red Horse Civil Engineering Squadron at Osan Air Base in South Korea sent over a team to work on everything from electrical and water lines, structural repairs to buildings and even repairs to a badly damaged runway.

When word of the killer earthquake made its way back to the United States, before long, Camp John Hay welcomed two civilian disaster assistance response teams. One of them deployed from Dade County, Florida and the other traveled all the way from Fairfax, Virginia.

Baguio became a city of tents for awhile. Baguio General Hospital, Notre Dame Hospital and St. Louis Hospital all had many tents erected on their property, several of the tents having been brought in by, and erected by, members of the U.S. Air Force's 90th Engineering Services Flight Prime Beef Team. Unfortunately, some area residents had to sleep outdoors in the chilly night air underneath substandard shelters made up of umbrellas, blankets and plastic sheets. And they were the lucky ones.


Ross thought he heard a familiar voice and opened his eyes. He hadn't been asleep, just resting. He wondered how anyone could get any sleep in this ward when doctors and nurses came into his room frequently to check on him, check his IV drip, bring him some pills to take and on and on and on, one interruption after another while trying his best to get some much-needed sleep. He was told that he'd been unconscious for two and a half days after he was brought in, then he woke up wondering where he was, how long he had been here, what were his injuries and if anyone knew if Maribel Edwards was OK. He was a light sleeper and he seemed to hear everything and everything seemed to keep him awake, especially the pain he felt all over his sore body. The pills could only do so much.

Doctor Edwards was standing next to his bed and a nurse was at the foot of it, writing something on his chart. "I didn't wake you up, did I?" Ross' former psychiatrist asked, in an apologetic tone.

"No, sir. I wasn't asleep. I was just resting. It's good to see you again," he said, speaking softly. "I have to talk low like this because when I tried to talk to one of the nurses in my normal voice, it made my head hurt, sort of like the way a hangover does."

Doctor Edwards nodded. "They tell me you were hurt pretty badly, a concussion, some cracked ribs, several bad contusions," he concluded, with a look of concern.

"Nothing that required any surgery. It will all heal in time. I'd say I was pretty lucky, all things considered," he said with a smile and once again speaking in a softer-than-normal voice. "Did Maribel make it out of the hotel OK?" He still had no idea that she had been seriously, almost critically injured. The nurses in ICU were only allowed to tell family members and wouldn't tell him anything about her. Doctor Edward's face looked too solemn for his liking and he sensed something was wrong.

"She's still in the ICU, just down the hall from you," the distraut father stated sadly. "They say that she'll be OK but I'm worried just the same." He was looking down and not directly at Ross and he had a far-away look in his eyes.

"What happened to her? The last time I saw her, she was in her hotel room getting ready to take me sight-seeing around Baguio. I went to my room down the hall to get my camera and that's when the earthquake hit and then something must have hit me in the head and knocked me out cold because I don't remember anything after that. How badly is she injured?" He was sincerely concerned about her well-being and it showed on his face as her father was now looking him in the eyes. There's no faking that kind of look and Doctor Edwards took notice of it.

"I don't know the details about how she got her injuries but she's in really bad shape. She has two black eyes that make her look like a creature that's half-racoon and half-human. With an oxygen mask on her face and tubes and IVs sticking out of her, it was hard for me to recognize my own daughter when I first saw her." He paused a moment and slowly shook his head back and forth as he saw the image of her in his mind. Ross just stared up at him in disbelief.

"She's got a bad concussion, a few broken ribs and contusions all over her body, bruises that are big, dark and ugly. It seems like you two have some of the same types of injuries, doesn't it?" he asked as he suddenly realized the coincidence.

"Yes sir, come to think of it, you're right. Maybe we had a wall collapse on us or something, I don't really know. My aching body sure feels like somebody dropped a ton of bricks on me. I'm covered in bruises too, mostly on my back and the back of my legs. I just got lucky and somehow came away from it all without the black eyes. My ribs were only cracked and not broken, but it's close to the same thing. I'm sure that Maribel will pull through it OK. She's young and strong and she's getting the best medical treatment anyone could hope for, right?" Ross tried to put a bright spot on an otherwise dim situation. Dear God, please help her get well again and recover from her injuries, he silently prayed.

"That's what one of her nurses said to me the other day, that she's young and strong. I know both the nurse and you are trying to give me hope and raise my morale and I appreciate it," he said, with a faint smile of thanks.

"Why don't you pull up a chair, Doctor Edwards?" Ross wanted to ask him some more questions about Maribel and their conversation was keeping his mind off the pain he was feeling, both of the body and the heart. The bad news about Maribel was bothering him in ways that had once bothered him for someone else in his life.

"No, I've got to get home, get something to eat and get some rest. I've spent so much time next to Maribel in the ICU that I've almost lost track of time and it's getting late. I'm glad to see you're at least conscious now and able to talk some. I hope you heal up fast. I'll stop in and visit again some time." With a wave of his hand, the doctor left Ross alone again, but not for long. Thirty seconds after he departed, another nurse came in to check his pulse and blood pressure and take his temperature. He couldn't wait to be well enough to leave, and not just the ICU either.

A day later and Ross almost got his wish, almost. He was transferred out of the ICU to a regular ward for recovering patients. After having his vitals checked again and his medical chart reexamined, he was given permission to walk around the hospital. After having been in bed for over a week, it took him a few steps before he felt steady enough to walk beyond his own ward. He did not feel comfortable wearing the hospital garb of pale green slippers and a light-weight pale green robe over loose-fitting pale green pajamas but he had no choice at the moment. Anyway, he was a man on a mission. He wanted to visit Maribel in the ICU and he was determined to try.

He was turned away when he asked to see her, told that only immediate family members were allowed to do that. However, his spirits soared when the nurse behind the desk near the entrance to the ICU informed him that Maribel might be moved to a regular room the next day or two as she was beginning to show some signs of improvement.

"I'm only telling you this," the nurse stated in a hushed voice as if she feared being overheard, "because Doctor Edwards told me that he thought you might come here and ask to see her and he gave his permission to let you know about her condition. You must be someone special, Captain Ross." She grinned up at him from her desk when she said that, as if she was implying something.

"I was their patient for awhile and I owe them a lot," he said, not wishing to add anything about the circumstances that led to he and Maribel both being in the hospital at the same time or about how he was once a patient of theirs. With a nod of his head to the nurse, he turned and slowly walked back to his room. He felt very happy at the news.

Two days later Ross was visited by Doctor Edwards again and was told where Maribel had been moved. She was now just a short distance down the hall from him, able to talk now. She was no longer hooked up to oxygen, monitors or IV tubes, much to her delight.

"I've got to warn you, Tom, she still looks terrible and she has a long way to go yet before she'll be released from the hospital. She's very self-conscious about how she looks with those two black eyes and ugly bruises all over her body," the concerned father stated. He wouldn't be a Colonel or a doctor forever but he would be a loving and caring parent for as long as he lived and Ross could tell from the way he talked about his only child, Maribel, no doubt about it.

"I'll keep my visit short," Ross promised.

"And there's one other thing, before I forget. Maribel asked me how you're doing. She still has the instincts of a doctor, you know, worried about her patient. Like father, like daughter, a chip off the old block," he chuckled as he left the room.

The next day, Ross quietly entered Maribel's room, afraid that she might be napping since he heard no sounds in it at all. The first thing he noticed was how much alike his room was to hers. The ever-present antiseptic smell, the TV mounted on a wall, facing the bed, the light pink-colored walls, the beige privacy curtain that hung on little rollers and could be closed around the bed and the emergency call button on the wall next to the bed as well. It was as if he'd just walked back into his own room by mistake. Even the floor-length, pale green curtains covering the windows on the far wall were the same as the ones in his room.

The only difference he could see, and it was impossible to overlook, was the large, clear glass vase on the nightstand, filled with a large bouquet of colorful flowers of all types and sizes, some in full-bloom, others in partial-bloom. Ross guessed that it was either a get-well gift from Maribel's father or her co-workers in the hospital.

The second-most colorful thing in the room was Maribel's face, poor thing. Ross couldn't very well overlook that either, thanks to the bright fluorescent lights, another common feature of his room and everyone else's in the hospital.

He just blurted out the first thing that came to mind, "I'm just happy as hell to see that you're alive and still in one piece," he told her, "forget about how you look. You'll heal up in no time and look just as pretty as you used to be. I mean, take a look at me!" Having said that, he removed the robe and then the pajama top he'd been wearing and, as he stood by her bed, mimiced a runway model during a Fall fashion show, turning around slowly and posing for her so she could see the many dark bruises on his battered and beat-up body.

She laughed at him and for the first time, smiled and felt no pain, but only momentarily. Laughing caused her ribs to hurt. "OK, OK, you made your point. Now put your clothes back on before someone sees you and throws you out of here. You're crazy, you know that?" The smile on her face was infectious and caused him to smile back at her as he put the shirt and robe back on.

"Well, I know a good psychiatrist who can help me regain my sanity. You up for the challenge?" he asked, happy to see that he had made her smile and forget her pain and injuries for a moment.

Just then a nurse walked in to check on her patient.

"Sorry to interrupt."

"That's OK, I was just leaving." Before Maribel had a chance to ask him to stay a little longer, he told her, "I'll come and check on you again tomorrow. Bye!" He was out the door in a few seconds, still moving slowly. He didn't like to drag out good-byes.

Ross had kept his visit with Maribel short, just as he'd told her father he would. It wasn't because she looked unattractive now, with her many injuries almost entirely changing her looks or the fact that she came right out and said how ugly she looked now and was embarrassed to be seen by him or anyone else. That was all just superficial stuff to him. It was just that he was a man of his word and since he'd told Doctor Edwards he'd keep his visit short, he kept his word and did just that.

Ross returned to his room and decided to try and take a nap. He also still had a long way to go in his recovery and his body was letting him know that now. He felt really tired and drained and in some pain.

Somewhere between daydreaming and sleeping, he thought back over his time in the Philippines so far, from the day he was first introduced to the medical intern, Maribel Edwards, until now. Grief counseling and psychoanalysis sessions, conducted almost entirely by her, had given him a new lease on life. He was no longer haunted by terrible dreams of an exploding bus and he no longer felt personally responsible for his wife's death because he didn't protect her and keep her safe as he had promised her father he would. He felt as if a giant weight had been lifted from him, and it had, both literally and figuratively.

Ross thought about all that he and Maribel had been through together, not just as patient and counselor but as a tourist and tour guide, as friends who'd been through a shooting and killing together and injured survivors of a powerful magnitude 7.9 earthquake that had killed and injured hundreds of people. It was as if the horrendous earthquake and aftermath had acted as a catalyst, providing a sudden epiphany about life, so simple and yet so hard to believe. Life was short and could be taken away from you at any moment, as it almost had for he and Maribel. How would he have felt if Maribel had died? He didn't even want to think about it.

He formed an image in his mind of what Maribel looked like just moments before the earthquake struck and ended their weekend sight-seeing plans. She was pretty, intelligent, cared about his psychological recovery and physical well-being, was a great travel companion and guide, translator and teacher of Philippine history and culture. He'd really enjoyed every single minute he'd spent with her except for the shooting in Cebu. He had to admit, that was down-right nerve-wracking. The rest of their time there was very enjoyable to him. Her injuries, like his, would heal and she'd be as pretty as ever once again.

He asked himself the same question about Maribel that he'd asked himself a few years before about Genevieve. What was there not to love about her? He finally admitted it to himself after much soul-searching. He loved Maribel, plain and simple. That was the truth of the matter, "the bottom line" as he called it and he couldn't deny it.

In the final analysis, he felt that he had everything to gain and nothing to lose by asking her to marry him. He was convinced that it was the right thing to do, what he really, deep-down, wanted to do. He was twenty-seven, she was twenty-four. No issues there, he thought.

The more he thought about it, he felt alive again, happy again, in love again. What better way to begin a new life, especially after their recent close calls with death? Rising from the ashes of his old life that had seemed to die with the death of his wife, Genevieve, in South Vietnam, he'd become a new man in the Philippines and it seemed to him, mainly because of Maribel.

Ross bought a beautiful diamond engagement ring at the Base Exchange the next day, guessing what ring size to get. It wasn't the largest stone they had, nor was it the smallest either. As he entered Maribel's brightly-lit hospital room, he thought how much it stood out in stark contrast to the small hotel balcony on a dark night, under a star-lit sky one evening in Saigon where Ross had proposed to Genevieve. Just as he had been then, he was really nervous now. His heart was beating a mile-a-minute. He was just glad that there was not another patient in the other bed in the room or someone from the medical staff either. He wanted this quiet moment with Maribel to be in total privacy.

She greeted him with a smile. "Hi! Come over here and have a seat so we can chat for a spell." Her father had been sitting in the chair near her bed less than an hour ago. "I see you're not in your hospital clothes anymore. Is that permanent or just temporary?" She was very happy to see him again. He'd made her laugh during his last visit, the first time she'd laughed since the earthquake and she really needed that. It uplifted her spirits more than he'd ever know. She loved his sense of humor, among other things. His bright hazel eyes were a close second.

"Just temporary, I'm afraid," he replied as he sat down in the chair she'd pointed to. "How are you feeling today?"

"I'm still sore all over but not as bad as last week. How about you?" She noticed that he had a nervous look on his face. She had seen his face so many times since they had first met that she could almost read his emotions just by looking at him. Something was different about him today, of that, she felt certain.

"Oh, I'm healing up, slow but sure. My doctor says I might even be able to return to limited duty by next week."

Then, after taking a deep breath and working up the courage, he began telling her what he'd been thinking the other day, about all the things they'd experienced together, starting back on "day one" as he referred to the day he began his first grief counseling session with her. He tried his best to explain his feelings towards her and why he felt the way he did and then surprised her with the "big question."

While listening to him, she realized that she shared many of the same feelings for him too, maybe not to the same level as he felt for her, but definitely the same kinds of feelings. She'd never told him about her feelings for him either because she hadn't convinced herself that it was the right thing to do or the right time to tell him either.

Maribel thought that she knew what this was leading up to but was still surprised anyway by the last four words Ross spoke, "Will you marry me?" as he showed her the sparkling diamond engagement ring, suddenly getting down on one knee, prepared to do things the old-fashioned way.

She no sooner looked wide-eyed at the ring when everything else became a fuzzy blur as her slightly almond-shaped, not-quite-round, brown eyes began to shed tears. She knew this man better than anyone she'd ever met before. He'd placed his body and his life between a gunman and her in Cebu, protecting her from possible injury or even death. Twice she'd felt his arm across her shoulders and felt comforted and safe. Everything he'd just said about how he felt about her was sincere and mirrored her own feelings about him and there was no denying it.

She managed to sob out a barely audible, "Yes," as she shook her head up and down, wiped away the tears and held up her left hand so he could slip the ring onto her finger.

Ross stood up and leaned over Maribel as she sat up in her hospital bed. He slid the sparkling diamond engagement ring on her finger and felt her other hand behind his head, pulling him to her for a kiss. It was their very first kiss, a long, lingering, passionate one. As for the ring, she loved it. It was a perfect fit.

## EPILOGUE

Before leaving the Philippines, Maribel Edwards finished her internship at the 13th Air Force Regional Medical Center at Clark Air Base and became a board-certified psychiatrist. Her proud father was on hand when she received that hard-earned honor and was there at her wedding, proudly walking her down the aisle of the base chapel where she and her husband, Air Force Captain Tom Ross, had a non-denominational service and wedding ceremony to the delight of all who attended.

The newlyweds rented a cabin at a place called Long Beach Resort, along the warm waters of the Lingayen Gulf for their honeymoon and decided right then and there to start a family.

Tom and Maribel Ross healed completely,

with no tell-tale signs of the injuries received from the devastating earthquake they had experienced together in Baguio. To Ross, Maribel was even prettier than before, after she became pregnant.

Doctor Melvin Edwards retired from the U.S. Air Force after thirty years of faithful service to his country and joined his daughter, son-in-law and grandson, Tim, in Los Angeles, California where they settled down after Ross left the Air Force to join a large company that conducted private investigations.

Mang Binh Hao was last seen in Hong Kong shortly before his wife had someone poison him to death so she could inherit his money and live very well-off with a young lover.

Bhoy Santos, Mang Binh Hao's Philippine connection, along with six of his gang members, died in a blaze of gunfire. They were all convicted of selling and distributing drugs, racketeering, murder and kidnapping with intent to commit murder. Under martial law, since they were caught with weapons while commiting the last crime, they were sentenced to death by firing squad.

Though Tom Ross was never able to find out the identity of any one particular person or persons responsible for the death of his first wife, Genevieve, and her uncle, he believed that it was the Viet Cong, at the urging of Mang Binh Hao, who blew up the passenger bus in the mistaken belief that he was on it. In the final analysis, Ross felt that the Viet Cong mistook Genevieve's French uncle, Pierre Ferrand, for him and that he was their main target all along, not Genevieve. It was Maribel who helped him come to that conclusion, mainly because of the incident in front of the U.S. Embassy in Manila. Ross had been the target of Bhoy Santos then, just as he had been the target of Mang Binh Hao back in South Vietnam. Ross had finally gotten around to telling Maribel everything about their trip to Manila and he felt better afterwards for having done so.

With the deaths of Mang Binh Hao and Bhoy Santos, fate had stepped in and helped settle some scores, just as fate had given Ross and Maribel a second chance at life.

## ABOUT THE AUTHOR

Steve Crews was born an Air Force brat and remained so until he began a 22-year military career in the U.S. Air Force in 1971. He spent many years traveling in all 50 states and 8 countries, including a year-long tour of duty in the Republic of South Vietnam and three tours of duty, adding up to $11\frac{1}{2}$ years in the Philippines.

He graduated from the University of the Philippines on May 31, 1981 with a Bachelor of Arts degree, majoring in Psychology, Sociology and Political Science.

He currently lives in Mississippi with over 500 other military veterans of World War II, Korea and Vietnam, some of America's most patriotic people, in the Armed Forces Retirement Home in Gulfport.

Printed in the United States
By Bookmasters